What early readers say...

"Kids, a dog, a four hundred year old mystery... add supernatural to the mix, and you're off on a wild adventure, where quick decisions and wit just may save a life. Faith Reese Martin's *White Doe in the Mist* should be on the reading list of any young readers who are looking for thrills and chills."

Nancy Slonim Aronie
author—Writing From the Heart and founder of the Chilmark Writing Workshop

"*White Doe in the Mist,* by Faith Reese Martin, is a winning combination of history, supernatural, and mystery. It's an adventurous romp from the present to the past and back again. Martin's breezy style will delight young readers as a twelve-year-old girl, a boy, and a Jack Russell terrier attempt to solve one of America's oldest mysteries."

Mike Klaassen
author—Cracks and The Brute for Young Adults

"With a trio of intrepid explorers leading the way, this spunky tale of mystery and history is sure to delight readers of all ages."

Maria V. Snyder
author—Poison Study and Magic Study

For more words from our readers see page XXX

JMP History Mystery Detective Series

White Doe in the Mist

Teen Jinx MacKenzie didn't acquire her nickname easily, and she has the bumps, bangs, and bruises to prove it. Her 'gift' of communicating with visitors from the past has Jinx and her friend Max using clues to help a frightened little girl from 400 years ago.

Ghost Train to Freedom

Jinx and Max travel the dark Time Tunnel to the past to attempt the most daring feat of their lives—a search and rescue using the most dangerous train in the world—the Underground Railroad.

COMING SOON

XXXXXXXXXXX

Two teen-age friends and their pets run a desperate race through the Time Tunnel of history. Their mission is to thwart a gang of ruffians who are intent upon murdering the last fourteen members of the Conestoga Indian tribe.

XXXXXXXXXXXX

Modern day pirates, Blackbeard, and eleven sunken treasure ships! Psychic teen friends Max Myers and Jinx MacKenzie have their hands full of problems when they become stranded back in time during the hurricane of 1715 ... and Blackbeard is NOT happy!

White Doe in the Mist

The Mystery of the Lost Colony

Faith Reese Martin

JMP History Mystery Detective Series

Book 1

American Literary Publishing is an imprint of LifeReloaded Specialty Publishing LLC
Lancaster, PA

White Doe in the Mist

American Literary Publishing
an imprint of LifeReloaded Specialty Publishing LLC
Lancaster, PA
www.americanliterarypublishing.com

Design and layout—Mike Lovell
Artwork—Larissa Hise Henoch
Cover art—John Votel
Editing—Lisa Hauser

ISBN: 978-1-60800-016-6
LCCN: 2012940647

Designed, published and printed in the United States of America

Dedication

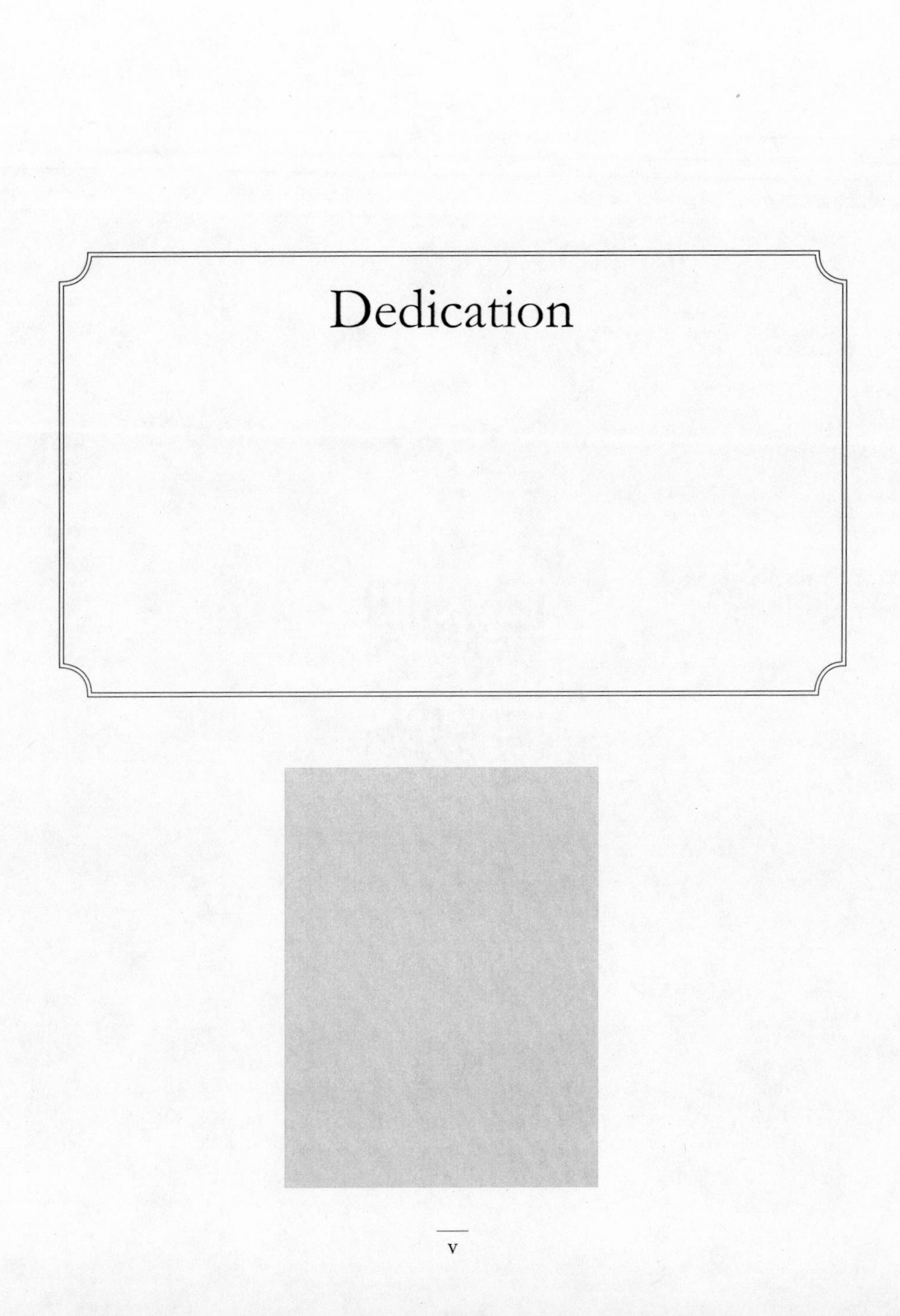

www.WhiteDoeInTheMist.com/historical

Visit the *White Doe in the Mist* website to discover more about the real history of the Lost Colony on Roanoake Island, NC:

Inspiration for White Doe in the Mist

Sincerely,

Faith Reese Martin

ACKNOWLEDGEMENTS

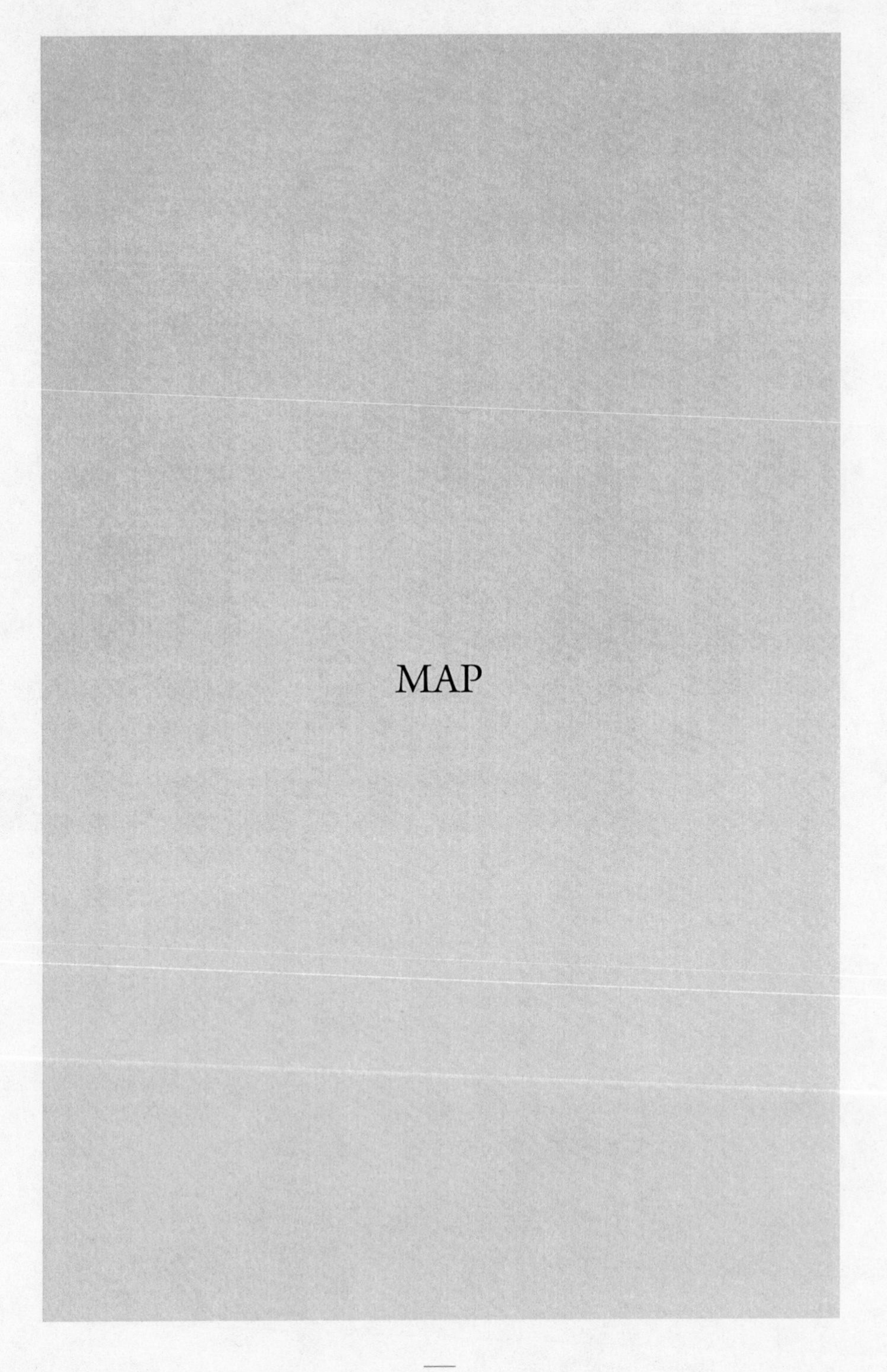
MAP

Contents

Prologue:

Aboard the Lyon

Seasick! I threw up in the wooden bucket and swiped at the sweat on my face with my sleeve, then skittered backward like a crab and pushed myself tight against the tarred, wooden sides in the bottom of the rolling ship. How on earth I got here was a mystery; a horrible nightmare jumbled in my feverish mind.

I gazed around me in disbelief. It was very dim, but I could see small groups of men, women, and children sitting and standing all around and talking in low voices. Some of the children cried in their mother's arms. It smelled dank and sour down here with other slop buckets full of vomit and bathroom waste that sat in a corner. I closed my eyes against a round of dizziness.

"Father, will we soon be there?" said a boy. "I'm so tired of dry old salt-beef and hardtack pieces of biscuits. I had to pick weevils out of my biscuit last eve."

Some things never change, I thought. Even kids hundreds of years ago wanted to know when they were going to get there. I almost smiled. I wondered where "there" was?

The boy's father nodded. "Aye, lad, we're soon there. I heard the sailors talking last night that land should be near." He patted his son's dirty head.

These people weren't from my time. It looked like I was in the midst of a movie cast filming some historical documentary. Only I knew these people were the real thing. They wore the clothing of sixteenth-century England, dresses and skirts that reached down to high-topped shoes, white blouses, breeches, long coats, and boots.

A dark-skinned sailor dressed in ragged pants and a striped shirt came partway down the steps from above and yelled, "Land, ho. Captain's orders are ye may come above if ye want to see us approach land." Then he turned back and disappeared.

A flurry of excitement rippled through the air.

"Land! After all of the long, treacherous weeks at sea," a young woman said. She held her arms folded over her swollen belly. "We are finally here, praise God!"

"You have been most brave, my love," said the young man at her side. "Who would have thought our new babe would be born in a new land? Our child will surely be remembered in history as the first English babe born in England's first colony in America."

An older man walked over to the young couple. "Yes, and we can thank our kind benefactor, Sir Walter Raleigh, for the opportunity to come build and live in his City of Raleigh. A new life in a land of plenty!" he said.

The woman hugged the older man. "Ah, Father, I am so excited to be here in America with you. To think Ananias and I will have hundreds of acres of land to farm...never in England could we have even dreamed of such a thing."

So, I was aboard a ship arriving at America hundreds of years in the past. This nightmare just got better and better I gave myself a mental shake. Wake up, wake up now, Jinx, I told myself. But I was already awake.

When the people rushed toward the wooden steps leading to the deck above, I pushed myself up and got in line. No one noticed a thin, redheaded girl. Good thing, too, since I looked totally out of place in the over-sized Phillies shirt, shorts, and flip-flops—a typical twelve-year-old from the twenty-first century.

Topside, I saw that I was aboard a three-masted sailing ship. There were sailors everywhere; some climbed the masts on rope ladders and some pulled on ropes attached to sails. The salty air filled my lungs, and I felt better.

"Trim the sails. Avast, mates, we head into the sound. Look lively," shouted a sailor, who looked like he was in charge.

He didn't look like a fair-skinned Englishman but rather he was darker-skinned. I edged over nearer to the man dressed in military splendor with his buttons and buckles shining in the sun. He wore a tri-corner fancy hat, a navy blue long-tailed coat and white pants tucked into shiny black boots.

The father of the woman below strode over to him, a frown on his face.

"'Tis Roanoke Island we need to find. That's where our soldiers were left last year, there in Fort Raleigh. We're to pick them up, Captain Ferdinando, before heading farther north to the Chesapeake Bay."

Ferdinando frowned back. "'Tis me that's the captain of the good flagship Lyon, and 'tis me who will decide where we sent anchor, John White."

John White's brows furrowed closely together. He looked as if he wanted to say more. Captain Ferdinando drew himself up very straight and glared at Mr. White—He scared me a little. I think he might have scared the Englishman, too.

With one last look at the captain, White turned and saw the others coming near. "Ah, my good colonist friends–feast your eyes on your new home, America." He swept his arm out toward the land jutting on the horizon. "Such a beautiful land to start anew ye'll not find anywhere else in the world."

The people cheered and clapped. I stared. Ok, someone rescue me, I thought. I felt like Dorothy in the Wizard of Oz. I was sure not in Kansas any more. Or Pennsylvania. I wondered if tapping my heels together three times and saying "there's no place like home" would wake me up. I took another shaky breath and tried not to burst into tears.

Something soft and furry brushed my left ankle.

"Jinx, touch me! I'll guide you home," said Petey, my beautiful Jack Russell terrier.

I was so happy to see him! "Oh Petey! Where have you be..."

"Aye, who are ye, then?" A sailor grabbed my wrist with his gnarly hand. He wore a red scarf tied around his head and a tattoo of a sea serpent slithered around the arm that clutched me. I

looked at his shifty eyes. He glanced around to make sure no one claimed me, then started to drag me with him.

"Capt'n wants for a new cabin boy since his other died of dysentery, so come with me, lad," he hissed between rotten teeth.

"Let go. I don't even belong here. Help!" I cried. And I'm a girl, anyway, you stinking pirate, I thought. I was more terrified than ever, but no one even heard me over the excitement of arriving in America.

Petey growled and snapped at the sailor's leg. "GRRrrrrrrr... let her go, you scurvy Pirate," he said.

The sailor shook his leg, but Petey hung on and flew back and forth through the air.

The sailor finally dropped my arm and grabbed his ankle. "Ouch! Ouch! Get away ye little cur!"

I picked up Petey and held him to my chest. I hid my face in his warm fur. "Help me, Petey, please..."

A cold, rushing wind grabbed me up and whirled me into a long, dark tunnel. What had just happened? Where was I going? I knew that my life was changing in some important way right then. I just hoped and prayed that it was changing for the better.

Chapter One:

Off We Go

"Booooo-rummmmm…!"

I leaned against the railing of the huge old ferry and listened to the deep, grumbling blast of her whistle. *Holy mackerel, loud enough for you?* I shielded my eyes from the sparkling glare of the sun on the water, and I wished for the millionth time that I hadn't left my sunglasses at the depot's lunch counter.

A ghostly image of an ancient sailing ship wavered on the horizon and captured my attention. I squinted my eyes to get a better look. It looked like the model of a British galleon that we had in our school library. The white sails glimmered above the water, and the smaller flags with a red cross, at the tips of the masts, snapped in the breezes.

"Excuse me, please," I said, to the woman who gazed out at the bay next to me. She was obviously a tourist with her camera strapped around her neck. "Do you see that sailing ship way out there? The one that looks like an old galleon?" I asked her. When we looked back out along the skyline, it was empty. She smiled at me and looked where I pointed.

"Do you mean those Sunfish?" she asked. I followed where she pointed to a line of colorful little modern watercraft.

I shook my head. Where had that galleon gone so fast? I guess my imagination had played tricks on me once again. Strange images and dreams bothered me often. I wished they would stop. I thought about the nightmare I had last week–I shuddered.

That short, terrifying excursion aboard a sailing ship the other night had scared me to death. Was it a nightmare? Was it real? Had I really traveled through time? And if I had, what did that make me? I felt kind of like...an alien. Sorta...creeped out. I mean who time travels? No one I know, that's for sure. But then again, who else talks with the animals, and they talk back? Oh, yeah! That's me, too.

I took a deep breath. The salty tang in the air, with a slightly fishy odor, always conjured up fond memories of the beach. It lifted my droopy spirits, if only for a few minutes.

I felt a soft, wet nudge against my leg and looked down into the dark, intelligent eyes of Petey.

"Sad, Jinx?" my furry friend asked me silently.

Petey always knows how I am feeling. I never could hide my emotions from him, so I didn't even try.

"Just in a bad mood, Petey. I'll be okay. You go back to your gull watching."

I sighed. Petey tilted his head, gave me a little lick on my ankle and scampered back to the starboard side of the deck to watch people throw popcorn to the gulls. So much for the "Do Not Feed the Gulls" sign.

"Love you, Jinx," floated back to me, in the salty breezes.

"Thanks, Petey. I love you, too."

Petey is the most beautiful Jack Russell terrier in the world. His brown and white coat is soft and shaggy, one ear usually at attention while the other droops, and his cute little stub of a tail is constantly wagging. He's not just any dog; he's my brother. The moment I met him as a tiny pup we connected forever.

It's mysterious how we can silently communicate. I've never told anyone, not Mom and Dad, or my best friends. No one else hears him. I'm pretty sure they'd lock me up somewhere for being a lunatic if I tried to tell people that I can talk to my dog—and, *oh, by the way, he talks back to me*—so I just keep this secret between Petey and me.

I knew I shouldn't be in such a dark mood, but I had plenty of reason for it. Both of my parents are archeologists. Mom's research on the Native Americans took us to Roanoke Island, in the Outer Banks of North Carolina, for the summer, while Dad traveled in Europe for his research.

That alone is not a bad thing. I love the ocean, but it didn't promise to be a relaxing, carefree summer at the beach for me. I miserably failed my final history exam and was in big danger of not passing sixth grade because of that one course. The teacher made a deal with Mom that if I researched and wrote an acceptable history paper during the summer break, I would pass.

No pressure! Humiliating, yes!?!! The daughter of history and archeology specialists, Margaret and Jeremy MacKenzie, fails her history course. I really let Mom and Dad down. *And* I had no clue what history topic to pick, much less any motivation to even write the doggone paper.

Petey threw me a look for using "doggone."

"Sorry, Petey, no disrespect meant."

Mom joined me at the rail and put her arm around my shoulders.

"Well, Jinx, what do you think? It's a beautiful day, and we're soon off to our beach cottage for some fun."

I gave a little shrug of my shoulders and kept my eyes on the deep green water lapping against the pier.

"Jinx, I'm worried about you. You haven't been yourself for weeks. I know you're almost a teenager, but if something is bothering you, you can still talk to your ol' mom."

"Sorry, Mom. I know I'm not good company. I guess I'm really worried about...everything. Failing my history test, disappointing Daddy and you, writing a good research paper for my teacher..."

I could see her concern when I looked into her kind, brown eyes. My mom and dad are gorgeous people, tall, dark, and handsome. Mom looked like a teenager herself, with her auburn hair pulled into a ponytail that stuck out the back of a Phillies cap. Mom always looks great, even without trying.

I feel like the ugly duckling compared to my parents. They look like Barbie and Ken dolls, and I look like E.T., their ugly little kid. I have bright green eyes, wild red hair spiking out all over, and I am all arms and legs that get tangled up most of the time. Does this sound like the offspring of Barbie and Ken?

"Jinx, you worry too much. You've never disappointed us. We know you can do better. And I'll be able to help you with that paper."

"But don't you see, Mom? That's the problem. You *like* to research and write papers. It's *easy* for you. You can't possibly understand how *boring* history is for me. I know you and Daddy love what you do, but I'm not like you. Maybe *I* have to be *me*," I said dramatically.

I pulled away from her and rolled my eyes. Then my shoulders slumped. *Ew! I even sounded like a whiner to me.* I took a deep breath and tried again.

"Mom, I don't even know where to start."

Mom smiled. "We-e-ll, I've got an idea for you. Would you like to hear about a four-hundred-year-old mystery that's never been solved? It happened right where we're going–Roanoke Island–where we'll be staying this summer."

The excitement in her voice made me turn to her again. She immediately waggled her eyebrows at me comically, as if to say, "it's really true."

A mystery on Roanoke Island? What had I heard about that before? I couldn't quite retrieve it. And Mom knows I love good mysteries. Okay, so I might have been a *little* interested, at that point.

Boooooo-Ruuum.

Yikes–we all jumped as the boat's horn wailed again, her last warning before departure from the harbor. I glanced around quickly to locate Petey.

"Excuse me, Mom. I can't see Petey...Petey, where are you? Oh no you don't!"

I caught a glimpse of the furry little clown dancing on his back legs with those cute front paws waving in the air. A family with a blue-eyed, blond boy about my age gathered around Petey. I could see they had been eating hotdogs and trying to keep the gulls away. My dog woofed to get their attention.

Petey leaped in the air, twisting like a gymnast in the Olympics, did a neat double roll over, then played dead. They burst out laughing and applauded, and the boy offered him a piece of his hot dog.

"Don't you dare, Petey. You know that you throw up every time you eat hot dogs." I called to him silently.

"But Jinx...I'm hungry."

"I'll be right back, Mom. I've got to go rescue those people from Petey."

Drat that Petey. He always got himself into trouble at the wrong time. I really wanted to hear about that Roanoke Island mystery.

I jumped over the short benches, then caught my sneaker in some rope and slid head first into the very cute, blue-eyed boy. *Tiiim-ber,* I thought, as he crashed to the deck in a tangled heap with me. The deck had been scrubbed down recently and still had some sudsy puddles that hadn't dried. I dried the deck for them, on my stomach.

The boy dropped the hot dog, and Petey, The Wonder Dog, grabbed it. He tore off with a silly smirk on his furry snoot, leaving me to disentangle myself and apologize.

I stood up soaking wet and tried to help the boy to his feet. He sat in a soapy puddle, gingerly checking his bruised knee. I felt like a total fool.

"Oh my gosh...oh gee...I am so sorry. I plowed you over, and my dog stole your hot dog, and...here, let me help you up."

Just then the boat gave a mighty lurch away from the dock, as we finally got under way. I lost my footing again and did a back end flop onto the deck again, facing the boy. *Niiiice,* I thought. *We might as well light a campfire and tell some stories. This is so embarrassing.*

"Maxwell M. Myers," he said, and offered his hand. "My friends call me Max. Those are my parents, Ward and June Myers." He thumbed toward the nice-looking couple that smiled down at us, and Max's parents waved. "Apology accepted. I believe this...er...unconventional...introduction should make us great friends. I love your dog. What kind is he?"

"He's a devilish Jack Russell terrier. I'm Margaret MacKenzie." I pumped his hand up and down. "But my friends call me Jinx. I guess you can tell how I got that nickname. This kind of crazy stuff tends to follow me around like a bad dream."

We got to our feet with our back ends dripping wet and laughed again. Max shook his long, blond hair back off of his face. I noticed that he was tall, thin, and very tan. He wore surfer beads around his neck. The freckles around his nose crinkled when he gave me a crooked grin.

"Well, I bet a lot of fun and good times follow you around too, Jinx. Come on, I'll help you lasso Petey, the Jack Russell *terror*."

This guy was okay. I knew then and there that I had a new friend. The summer looked better by the minute.

Chapter Two:

The Chase

Max and I took off at a run and tried to get a glimpse of Petey. The boat had two decks. Below, the cars and vans drove onto the boat to ferry across the sound. The upper deck offered benches, seats, hotdogs, and a view as sparkling as my new friend's blue eyes.

What is the matter with me, crazy over a boy? I rather liked this new and different feeling. Seems like this is going to be a summer of all kinds of new events for me, I thought. I smiled to myself.

"Over there, by the stairs," Max yelled. "I see the little fur ball heading below deck." He did a neat slide down the stair railing, and I followed.

Dodging in and out of the multitude of brightly colored vehicles, we tried in vain to catch up with Petey. Gone, fast as lightening.

"Petey, you hairy little doggie demon. Stop...come...sit..."

"Ha, Jinx. Try to catch me."

Jack Russell terriers have way too much energy and smarts. Plus, they can out run a locomotive.

"Boy, he is full of himself, isn't he?" laughed Max. "He's taunting you."

I threw a quick glance at Max as we ran and wondered if he somehow knew what Petey was saying to me. But, that wasn't possible, right?

When we got to the bow, no sign of Petey existed. We skipped up the rear stairs to the upper deck and stood there panting and trying to catch our breath.

In my active mind I pictured the worst. *Petey, knocked silly when he ran into the side of a van...Petey, heaving violently as he became sickened by the hot dog...Petey, calling out to me for help as a giant sea gull carried him off into the air. Oh please, get a grip,* I told myself.

We slowed down and walked around the deck once more. When we rounded to the port side we found Petey, rather green in the face. He sat in the middle of a coiled pile of rope and wobbled with each roll of the boat on the waves.

"Jinx, help me. I feel sick."

"What did I tell you?" I shot back.

Then I relented as I got a real look at my furry buddy. He looked so pitiful and miserable. With his soft little ears down, and his stubby tail tucked under him, he rolled his brown eyes toward me. My heart melted.

"Oh, Petey Buddy, we'll see if Mom has any of that pink stuff to settle your stomach," I communicated silently.

"If your mom doesn't, I know my mom has some," Max said. He looked at me with a mischievous smile.

O-kaaaay...what just happened here, I wondered. *He acts like he heard Petey and me communicating silently.* I tried an experiment.

"Max, can you hear what Petey and I are talking about?" I questioned him silently.

"Uh-huh," he returned in silence.

This is not a good thing, I thought to myself.

"Ahhh...can you read my thoughts, even when I'm not talking with Petey and you?"

"Only if you want me to. I don't seem to tune in very clearly unless Petey is involved."

Whew, what a relief. I had been terrified for a few seconds that he had heard all my girlie, lovey-dovey thoughts when I first met him.

"Wow, I've never run into anyone who could animal communicate like me," I said, aloud. "I'd always felt really alone with this...um... strange talent."

"Yeah, this is great!" said Max. "I never expected to find anther person in the world with this mystical talent. We're like Doctor Dolittle and his talking animals."

He reached up and absentmindedly tugged at a lock of his blond hair, then continued, "Mine started at an early age. I found myself understanding what my dogs and cats were thinking. Actually, it was more than that. I realized they spoke to me and wanted me to respond. So I tried it, and it worked.

"I used to forget myself and talk back to the animals out loud," Max added. "One time at the zoo I got some strange looks from people. When the monkeys told me I looked like an orangutan, I told the monkeys out loud to stick some bananas in their ears. I also made the mistake once, in third grade, of telling my best friend that I could talk with animals. He, of course, did not believe me, but he told me he liked me even if I was crazy."

"You know, this silent communication could come in handy if we ever get in trouble," I told Max. I didn't realize at the time how true those words would be.

"Help...help...too much yakking. I feel really bad," said Petey.

"Sorry, Petey." We both answered at the same moment.

"What goes up the chimney?" I shouted.

"Smoke," replied Max.

We hooked pinkie fingers, and I finished the old charm. "May your wish and my wish never be broke." It had to rhyme, even if my language arts teacher would cringe.

I closed my eyes and made my simple wish. I wanted to have some fun, mystery, and excitement this summer. Oh yeah, with my new friend included, I amended. I opened my eyes as Max scooped up Petey. We headed up to the stern where I had left Mom.

"Come on, Petey, you Hot Dog," Max said. He cradled him in his arms. "Let's get you some first aid." Petey gave him a look of pure adoration.

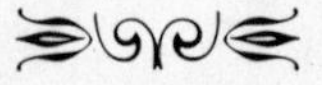

A little while later we sat on a hard bench in the sunshine and sipped on some ice-cold soda. We swung our legs and relaxed in a quiet, comfortable way. I felt like Max was a good buddy from school, like I had known him forever. I introduced him to Mom, and I could tell she liked him right away as she chatted with him.

Petey curled up in a tight little ball at my feet and took a snooze. He'd told me that he felt much better.

Max told me his family had rented a seaside cottage that sat just over the dunes from mine. We whispered all kinds of plans to sneak out late at night to explore the beach and collect shells early in the mornings. We planned to hike over to the lighthouse and climb the spiral stairs to the top. Max even volunteered to help me do some research for my paper.

"Sknxxxx...snortle... ZZZzzzzz..."

We laughed softly at the sounds of Petey's snores. Both of us watched the twitches his paws and legs made when he chased phantom sandpipers on the dunes of his dreams.

"So Mom, what's all this about a mystery on Roanoke Island?" I said.

"Are you talking about the Lost Colony, Mrs. MacKenzie?" Max asked. "I remember in the fourth grade we studied about England trying to colonize America so they could lay claim to more land, because Spain already had claimed the southern area of America. A small group of English colonists tried to make a go of it on Roanoke Island. They had a really rough time, though, and something happened to them, right?"

"Good job, Max," Mom said. "You're right on target."

Jeeze Louise, I thought. What is it with the whole world loving history? But I had to admit that I felt some strange connection to this story.

Booo-Ruuummm.

The good old ferry gave a blast of her whistle to alert the sailors on the dock to make way as she approached. Her massive engines cut back, and we could feel her slowing down. The propellers churned the harbor water into a creamy froth as the captain adeptly turned her around so he could back her into the dock. People chattered louder and scurried to gather their belongings and round up their kids.

Petey startled and jumped a mile high when the horn sounded, then yawned and stretched out on his belly with his back legs straight out behind him. He stretched his head and neck into the air with a silly grin on his face and pulled himself forward with his furry brown and white paws. Then he rolled over on his back and whipped back and forth like a break-dancer.

"Ahhhhh. I Feel good. Pink stuff worked."

"What on earth is he doing?" said Max. "He looks like some kind of snake-in-the-grass that went crazy."

"Yeah," I said, "we call that his Snake Dog–Roley Poley routine."

"I'll tell you what," Mom said, "why don't we have a campfire on the beach tomorrow night? We'll be unpacked and moved in by then. Max, you're invited if it's all right with your parents. I'll tell you two the mystery story about England's Lost Colony then, but beware. Some people say there are ghosts from long ago still roaming the island dunes and woods."

"Oh, Mom," I groaned. "You know I'm too old to be scared by some old ghost story."

"That's a great idea, thanks," said Max. "I know it'll be okay with my parents. I'll bring the hot dogs."

"No, noooo...no more hot dogs. Petey is sick of hot dogs." Petey rolled his button eyes and covered his face with his paws.

Max and I burst out laughing.

"What?" asked Mom.

"Oh, nothing, Mom. Petey just looks so silly."

Mom studied Petey and the two of us with raised eyebrows. I saw a question in her laughing eyes.

"You know, Jinx, sometimes I could swear that you and that silly dog actually talk to each other," Mom said.

This time Max and I covered our faces with our paws to stifle our laughter.

Chapter Three:

A First Connection

When the ferry docked, we hopped into our red Jeep Cherokee and waited for our turn to drive down the ramp back onto good old terra firma. We had ferried from Knots Island over the Currituck Sound to the village of Currituck just for the fun of a free ferry ride. I had a great time, but I wasn't so sure about Petey.

"Jinx, do we have to go back on the ferry? I'm seasick."

"No, Pete-o. I'll make sure we take the scenic land route. I guess you aren't going to become my salty old sea dog during this adventure?"

"Not if I have to go out on a boat."

I patted his head and gave him a big hug.

"Petey, you're the best buddy I've ever known. Promise me you'll be careful at the beach this summer. No swimming unless I'm along. And no solo jaunts."

"I love swimming in the waves, chasing crabs, and digging big holes in the sand," said Petey.

"Yeah, until a crab bites off your big nose for bugging him."

Petey wiggled all over with barely contained excitement. I could tell I'd have to keep a close eye on my furry brother to keep him out of danger. Looking back, I should have known it would be the other way around.

We waved good-bye to Max and his family when we left the ferry. They would be doing some sightseeing and wouldn't get to Roanoke Island until the next day. Max and I gave each other a thumbs-up. I caught his wide grin as he hopped into their maroon-colored family van.

"See you soon, Jinx. Petey, do not let that girl out of your sight. She's liable to get eaten by a great white shark," he silently commanded.

"Aye, aye, sir. Petey is on duty, sir.

He gave Max a smart salute with one hairy paw.

Hmmm, he never did that before. Maybe he'll turn into a salty old sea dog yet.

We headed down the beach highway for Point Harbor. Once there, we crossed over to the Outer Banks' Bodie Island. Mom had decided to cram some history down my throat this summer and felt there was no time like the present.

First we stopped at Kitty Hawk and Kill Devil Hills, the former summer home of the Wright Brothers. As we approached the site, a large visitors' center for the Wright Brothers National Memorial loomed into view. Nearby, on top of a huge dune, sat one of the most beautiful memorial monuments I've ever seen.

Large, sandy dunes covered the whole area. I didn't know they grew them that big. They even impressed Petey. For once he didn't run around in circles or jump off of all fours. I noticed four stone markers placed in a long line at the base of a dune and wondered why they were there.

We both froze at the same time as we gazed out over the shimmering dune. *Suddenly, a heavy sense of strange eeriness hung in the air, as if something awesome would happen there on that dune at any moment.* Petey snapped out of his stupor first and cocked his head in my direction.

"Jinx, Jinx. Run up and down the dune?"

"Not yet, Fur Face. I'm sure Mom wants us to look around the Visitors' Center and museum first."

"Ok...fine." His tail lost some of its wag.

"Now, now, Pete-o. One bad attitude in this tour group is enough. And that would be my job. Besides, we need a snack."

Mom walked up beside us. "Your history question for the afternoon is, what can you tell me about the Wright Brothers?" Mom asked, as she walked up beside us.

"Mom, I may not enjoy history, but I'm not totally stupid."

Mom gave me "THE LOOK" that said I better not push my luck, so I tried to make my tone a little more respectful.

"Uh, let's see. They made bicycles and liked to fly kites and gliders and...ummmm...I know. They made some airplane, but I don't know why that's such a big deal," I finished.

Mom nodded. "Good job, Jinx. But there's a little more to it than that. Let's get out of this hot sun and have a sandwich and some lemonade. The deal is, you go through the museum displays on your own and do a little research on the Wright Brothers. Then, you and Petey can head back outside to tour the grounds. I'll meet you at the top of the dune by the monument in an hour. Of course, by then, you'll be able to give me a few more facts."

"What is this Mom, a pop quiz? It's summer vacation, not school," I said.

"No, Jinx, this is known as a teachable moment. Off you go. And Petey, try to behave yourself."

Petey and I shared a bologna sandwich and an ice-cold bottle of spring water from our cooler, and I thought about flying free as a bird. It would be wonderful to take off from the top of the dune and sore through the clouds.

I took a quick peek in the gift shop. I love gift museum gift shops–they were always the best part of school trips. There were model planes, tee shirts, and puzzles. A brightly colored Hawaiian shirt on a rack caught my eyes. It was blue and had these flying machines and palm trees all over it. My Dad would love that shirt.

I marched toward the museum, determined to learn something new. To my surprise, a lot of interesting things caught my attention right away. We wandered through a scene of the Wright Brothers' bicycle shop filled with old tools and old-fashioned bicycles. Some of the bikes had no brakes. They must have worn down a bunch of shoes stopping them just by dragging their toes. Another bike had one giant front wheel and a tiny rear wheel. Way up high sat a skinny seat attached to a dull metal bar that curved down to the ground.

I pictured myself with my wild hair, in baggy polka dotted pants and a big red clown nose, perched way up there. I'd love to try riding around the ring in the Barnum and Bailey's Circus on a Wright Brothers' bicycle.

We strolled by replicas of work sheds that the Wright brothers built in the gritty sand during the summers and falls of the early 1900's. Camping gear, tools, kites, wooden frames, and cloth to make fancy hang gliders filled the sheds.

Old photographs showed the brothers as boys, playing in the yard of their family home. Their house reminded me of my aunt's comfortable, old farmhouse.

Suddenly, that heavy eeriness that I had felt outside filled the air around me. My attention seemed to be drawn to one particular photo of the brothers. It pictured them as grown men sitting on their back porch stoop.

They looked handsome in their old-fashioned gray suits and ties. Wilbur sat relaxed with his arm across his knee as he gazed out into the distance. He had a serious, far-away look on his face. He appeared to be deep in thought. I wondered what he had daydreamed about while that picture was taken.

For some reason, I felt drawn to Orville. He faced the camera and had his legs crossed with his hands clenched in front of his knees. Orville had on fancy, two-toned shoes and plaid socks. But it was his face that held my attention. He had really big ears like an elephant's, which stuck straight out. A giant handlebar mustache tickled his lips. The picture looked... comfortable. I thought that I would really like him as a friend.

All of a sudden I felt dizzy. Fog swirled around the picture. Petey started gently woofing at the photo. Then, Orville didn't just look into the camera, he looked right into my eyes. Orville seemed to be tired, and he had a sad little smile for me.

The photo got a bit fuzzy, and I blinked my watery eyes. Orville sat right there in front of me like he wanted to tell me something. My knees shook a little, and my stomach felt like knotted string. The moment passed, and my focus went back to the whole picture.

Petey woofed at Orville's picture again and wagged his stubby tail. He liked Orville.

"Come on, Petey, let's look around some more. That picture freaked me out."

"Orville is very smart. And nice," Petey informed me. Like he knew Orville personally...?

I gave Petey a quizzical look but kept going. Then I pulled up short in front of a plaque that read:

"Wilbur and Orville Wright are the flying force behind the miracle of the modern airplane. They successfully built the first plane capable of flying a man up into the blue skies. They experimented many years until they finally found the right combination of engine, wings, and propeller to make the aircraft fly. The perfectly balanced miracle machine, capable of soaring into the skies, took its first sustained flight on December 17, 1903, here at Kitty Hawk. Mankind became airborne."

I felt stunned. Now I got it–they were the very first people to build a *successful,* modern airplane. I wondered, *where was their take off point?* I needed to see more.

"Petey, time to check out that big old dune now. Last one to the top is a monkey's uncle."

"You lose, Jinx. You're a big monkey's uncle."

We tore off; our six feet flew and kicked the fine sand high into the air. The stiffening offshore breezes clutched at the sand and turned it into whirling dervishes, sending it on its way.

Gasping, with sand in my eyes, I galloped up the path of the hundred-foot high sand dune. *No Petey in sight. Ha. I finally left him behind in my dust.* Staggering over the crest of the dune I saw Fur Face. He sat calmly by the monument. His tail made an angel wing in the sand as his whiskery face greeted me. And he wasn't even winded.

"Jinx is a monkey's un-cle, a big monkey's un-cle," he sang, in his off-key doggie voice.

I sank to the ground to catch my breath, grabbed Petey, and tickled his belly. We flopped around like a couple of sand-colored ghost crabs being tossed head over heels by the breaking surf.

"And you're the big monkey who has an uncle. Now let's go see what that monument says," I said.

I didn't see Mom yet, so I walked around the monument studying the inscriptions. Aha. This was the actual dune where they made their first successful flight so many years ago. Their first four jump-off points were pegged with those stone markers I had seen when we arrived. But the dune had shifted over the years so that the take off spot and distance markers were now on flat ground.

Impressive! The Wright Brothers, our very own guys here in good old America, had invented and flown the first successful airplane. I felt a strange excitement deep in my stomach, like the butterflies you feel before you take a big leap into space. I grabbed Petey and tickled him again.

We walked further out on the ridge of the dune to catch more of the view. In one direction we saw whitecaps on the choppy ocean, and behind us lay endless sand, shimmering shadows, and dunes covered with scrub brush.

A strange wind really whipped up now, obscuring most of our view with flying sand. The monument disappeared, and I began to feel turned around and lost.

A huge black cloud covered the sun. I looked up into the darkened sky through the mini sandstorm and caught the shadow of an antique airplane. That's funny. It looked like a model of Wilbur and Orville's first airplane, the one that worked. I didn't know the museum had a flying exhibition today. A small, dark figure lying prone at the controls saluted us and dipped the wings of the plane back and forth. Then it disappeared.

What was going on? I felt dizzy and sweaty, as if I had the flu. My hand flew to my forehead to wipe away the sweat, and I fell to my knees.

Through the blowing, stinging curtain of sand a tall figure approached. Petey wagged his whole body as he barked a greeting. Since Petey trusted the person, I felt fairly safe. As the person got closer, I saw a man about Dad's age. He wore blue jeans and a loose, blue Hawaiian shirt covered with palm trees, clouds, and flying machines.

"Could you point me in the right direction to get back down the dune to the visitors' center?" I asked him in relief. I knew Mom would come looking for us there.

He nodded politely. I noticed he had very big ears that stuck straight out from his head, just like an elephant's. He also had a big handlebar mustache that tickled his lips, kind brown eyes, and a sad smile on his face. My eyes about popped out of my head.

I realized I stood there in the sand storm staring at him with my mouth wide open. I coughed from the sand and held my hands above my eyes, trying to shield them for a better look.

Petey walked over and put his legs up on the man's leg so he could lick his hand. The man stroked Petey's head, then handed me a huge, old-fashioned bandanna to hold over my mouth and nose for protection.

"Th..Thanks," I stuttered. "I'm sorry for staring, but you look just like...I mean, did anyone ever tell you...um... you look just like Orville Wright?"

He smiled and held up his hand to stop my stuttering, then motioned me to follow. A few steps in the opposite direction from where I had been heading he pointed down the dune through the flying, swirling sand.

"Thank you so much," I almost cried with relief.

As I looked downward I could see the outline of the visitors' center again. Then I remembered my manners. I turned to give back the expensive handkerchief that he had so graciously offered.

"And thanks for the use of this beautiful silk bandanna. I appreciate your help. When the sand storm started we got lost and..."

I looked at my rescue angel in the Hawaiian shirt. His deep-set brown eyes drew my attention. I couldn't help myself–I stared. Our eyes locked, and the moment stood still, frozen in time. I realized this was the real Orville Wright standing in front of me. It made me smile to see Orville wore a Hawaiian shirt. He must have visited the gift shop. He had probably worn modern clothes so he wouldn't frighten me.

The wind dropped, and the sand storm quieted. The sun broke out again. All was calm and beautiful. The rocks far below muffled the crashing of the ocean waves.

In that spellbound moment, I heard the gulls calling as they glided through the brilliant blue sky, just like the Wright Brothers' plane must have done one hundred years ago. In Orville's eyes I saw the gulls as they majestically soared toward the horizon. I pictured their dull-colored yellow bills and the black feathers on the tips of their white wings. I saw their piercing, black eyes and the sunlight reflecting off their bright feathers. Then they morphed into beautiful antique airplanes flying higher and higher until they were tiny black specks in the sky.

"Miss, I have an important message for you," said Orville. *"Don't be afraid of these new, mysterious powers. You are one of the few who are able to communicate with the past. The reason why will become apparent as you follow your destiny back in time. Let me show you some scenes from my past. Are you willing to go?"*

"Can Petey come along with me, Mr. Wright?" I said. This was almost too much for me to handle.

"Of course he may. Hold him tightly in your arms." Orville smiled at me.

Petey jumped up in my arms and put his soft face on my shoulder. He wiggled with excitement.

"It's okay, Jinx. It's safe with Orville. Time to learn about your powers," Petey said.

"Petey, you knew I had weird powers and didn't tell me?" I couldn't believe it.

"Wasn't time yet, Jinx. Relax–you'll be fine," said my furry little companion.

"Relax...*yeah, right*. Okay, sir, I'm ready," I barely whispered to Orville.

Orville put his hand on my shoulder, and the day immediately disappeared into a dark and cold tunnel. A whooshing wind seemed to pick us up and swirl us away. Would I return to ever see my mom and dad again?

Chapter Four:

The Boys of Dayton, Ohio

I stood in the yard of a large, white house. Petey jumped down and ran toward the front porch. I knew this place–it was Orville's and Wilbur's home from the picture in the museum. Orville was no longer with me. Two women walked by me on the sidewalk just a few feet away; they ignored me, chatting about the sunny day and getting home to start supper preparations.

"Hello," I said to a boy with big ears and sandy brown hair who ran into the yard.

The boy was dressed in the high-topped shoes, black stockings, and brown knickers of time long past. He ignored me as he almost tripped over his untied shoelaces. He knelt down to tie them. I walked over and tapped him on the shoulder, but my hand went right through him, as if he were made of fog. I jerked my hand back. Oh my...this was as bad as that dream about the sailing ship. I felt a tremor of icy fear tickle the back of my neck.

Another older boy opened the front door and yelled, "Orv, where have you been? Papa's brought us a new toy. Wait 'til you see it!" The screen door slammed shut as he disappeared back inside.

"Comin' Will," Orv shouted. He ran the rest of the way up to the porch. I ran with him, curious to see the new toy. The screen door slammed in my face as I glided right on through it into the living room. Interesting, I thought. I'm obviously an unseen observer, and I can go through walls... Okaaay, that was too weird.

Something came flying through the air, with Petey chasing it at full throttle. He leapt into the air and knocked it with his paw. His paws went through it, like my hands had gone through Orville's shoulder. It bounced off of Orv's shoulder to the floor. No one knew that a wild little Jack Russell terrier tried to grab the toy out of the air.

Laughing children filled the room. They must be Orville's and Wilbur's brothers and sister, I thought. Something inside me clicked like a switch. These were real people from the past. I was actually seeing the Wright family, even if they couldn't see Petey and me. Real people! Real history!

"Petey, get over here, and sit by me. You'll break the toy if you do that; it's only made of bamboo and paper stuck into a cork," I said. Petey listened like a good dog.

"But I can't really catch it...too bad," Petey said.

"Oh, right," I said. Well, stay here with me anyway. I'm a little, um, scared."

Petey moved tighter against me. I loved that little guy.

Orv picked up the toy and studied it, with a creased brow and cocked head. "It's a whirligig that flies," he said. He held the bamboo stick in his left hand while he twisted the foot long rotor blade attached to a rubber band as tightly as it would go.

"Ready, set, go!" Orv shouted, as he raised his arm and let it fly.

It was all too much for Petey to remain sitting. Away he flew with the children as they chased it around the room.

A laughing woman came into the room from the kitchen to see what was going on. She shook her head at her rambunctious children. The whirligig hit a table lamp by her side. She managed to grab the lamp before it crashed over to the floor.

"All right, children, you all go experiment with the whirligig outside where it can't do any damage," she said.

A man stuck his head out of a study. "Yes, a little peace and quiet, please," he said, in good humor. "I'm trying to finish the newspaper for the church. It's a big responsibility being Bishop for the church. Too much work, and not enough time for fun. I wish I could join you," he said.

"They're going outside, Milton. Right children?" said their mother.

"Yes, Father. Sorry, Father," said lots of voices, as they giggled and pushed.

The oldest boy picked up the toy, and most of the children followed him outside.

Orv grabbed his brother by the shoulder and said, "Wait, Will. Did you notice how the whirligig tilted a bit to the side? I wonder, if we could twist the rotor blade a bit–maybe that would straighten up the flight."

Wilbur nodded his head. "Show me what you mean on paper," he said.

The boys went to the dining room table, which was covered with paper and pens and inkpots. Diagrams and pictures of different machines had been carefully drawn on sheets of paper, lying beside metal pieces and springs. The table was also littered with bamboo strips, cloth, and balls of string, the items needed to make a kite.

Orv grabbed a feather pen and dipped it into the inkpot. Before he started his sketch, he paused and looked at his big brother.

"Um...Will, you won't tell Mother that I got into trouble for dipping Becky Mather's pigtail into the ink pot? I just meant it as a joke."

Wilbur grinned at his brother. "You're sweet on her, aren't you? Now I know why you were late getting home today. Had to stay after and scrub the chalkboards and clean the desktops, didn't you? No, your secret's safe with me."

Mrs. Wright quietly followed them into the room. I saw her smile to herself. It was becoming obvious to me that Orville was the most mischievous of all her children.

"So, tomorrow morning you'll be up early picking some apples to give Teacher and Becky Mather, along with an apology to both," Mrs. Wright scolded. She reached over to ruffle her son's hair.

Orville ducked his head and blushed as red as the apples he was to pick in the morning. "Yes, Mother. Sorry."

The attractive woman's brow drew together at the sight of a mantel clock lying in pieces on the table. "Oh, Orville! Not your grandfather's clock. It belonged to my father..."

This time, Will blushed. "We wanted to see how it worked, Mother. We'll put it back together, really," Will said. Orv nodded.

Both boys were soon huddled over their drawings as they planned a better whirligig–one that would fly straighter and stay in the air longer.

Petey jumped into my arms, and I felt a hand on my shoulder. Grown-up Orville smiled at me. The scene faded away.

"One more story," Orville said. "Ready?"

I had to laugh as I thought about him misbehaving in school. Orville shrugged his shoulders. "Becky was a very pretty girl," he admitted.

The cold tunnel sucked us in. I felt like the whirligig as I swirled through the darkness. Oh, my stomach...

Petey and I tumbled onto a large sand dune, beside what look like a sixty-foot long wooden track. I glanced back over my shoulder and saw the Wright Brother's 1903 Flyer, resting on a wooden dolly on wheels. I didn't have to be a genius to figure out where Petey and I had traveled to: we were near Kitty Hawk, in Kill Devil Hills, North Carolina, but this was way before the monument and Wright Brothers Museum were built. This was the real thing–the day Wilbur and Orville tried out their Flyer to see if they could actually take to the air. I was invited to attend!

Petey danced in the sand around the biplane, and I studied the Flyer. It had a set of two long cloth wings with wooden struts and wires strung between them. Hmmm... I wondered what the wires were for? Two short wings were attached in front, and what looked kind of like a rectangular box kite was attached perpendicular for a rear rudder. Two wooden propellers were behind the two big wings. The propellers had chains to move them, like bicycle chains.

Wow, this wasn't just a big glider–it had an engine and gas tank, and some wooden controls. The Wright brothers really meant business.

I thought about how much the brothers had learned from their boyhood days of experimenting with whirligigs and kites. I read in the museum that their bicycle shop helped them learn about air and flight also, when they experimented with lightweight bicycle frames built to speed through the air and help them win races back in Dayton, Ohio. With the Wright boys, it always had been a fascination with air and flight.

Both Wilbur and Orville hiked over the ridge to the top of the dune where their Flyer awaited. They were dressed in woolen pants and jackets and caps, because the day was cold and windy. Again, I knew they couldn't see Petey and me. We were lucky observers.

A few other men and a boy plodded up the shifting sand of the dune. One man set up a camera on a tripod.

"Well, boys, this could be it!" said the man with the camera. "I'll capture the first flight with my camera. I have a good feeling about it. Today the flight will go off without a hitch."

The boy was so excited that he jumped around the plane, like Petey. "Thanks, Mr. Wright, thanks to both of you for letting me watch you practice with the gliders this fall. My mother sent an apple pie for you today. She said I wasn't to be in the way, but I told her you never minded me coming over to see you. Wow! The Flyer–she looks swell. I know she'll fly like a bird." He gazed amazement at the flying machine. Three days ago, Wilbur had crashed and damaged the wings. But the Flyer looked good as new, today.

Wilbur looked concerned. He wet his thumb and held it up into the stiff breeze. "It's really blowing today; where's that French anemometer?"

"An-a…an-a-mom…what's that, Mr. Wright?" asked the boy.

"Ah, here it is," Wilbur said. "Come here, son, see how these cups spin in the air? They're attached to a gear that makes this gauge needle move. Watch…" He held it straight up to catch the wind.

"Whoa, the cups are flyin' around…it's pointing at twenty-seven. Does that mean the wind is blowin' twenty-seven miles per hour?" asked the boy.

"That's right," Wilbur said. "Stiffer wind than I'd like, but it's already December 17th; we're running out of time for the year. We've come so close to actual sustained flight. What do you say, Orv?"

"I say, it's my turn to fly, since you flew three days ago–let's go for it," Orville said. He gave everyone the two thumb-up sign as he walked with confidence to the bi-plane and crawled into the framework. They had learned more about controlling the Flyer every time they had tried a flight.

Again the excited boy ran over to see how Orville fit into the frame. "It looks real hard to do, sir. I don't think I'd ever understand how this flyin' machine works," he said.

Orville chuckled at the boy's enthusiasm. "Flight is actually pretty simple, son. To fly, the plane needs three things, just like the seagulls. It needs lift. The wings provide lift. That means the air going over and under the wings has to be just right. It needs thrust–that means forward motion. The gulls can flap their wings to move forward, but our flying machine has these propellers spinning around to do that job. The last thing needed is control, and that was the hardest thing to get right. We want to be able to go up and down, and go left and right in the air. So I have this wooden lever to move those little front elevator wings, see?"

Orville wiggled the hand lever, and I saw the boy's head go up and down like the front wings as Orville worked the lever.. He gasped.

"I see, Mr. Wright! I see how they move," said the boy.

"Now look at this wooden cradle here by my hips," said Orville. Watch when I wiggle my hips." He started wiggling like Petey does when he crawls across the ground. The wires between the two large wings bent the wings up and down, back and forth.

Even I could understand how it worked. "I get it, Petey. I finally understand how planes work: lift, thrust, and control," I whispered in his ear. He wiggled and yipped his agreement.

"Everyone, clear the Flyer's path. Here we go," said Orville. Wilbur started the engine, while Orv laid low, and pulled his wool cap tighter over his ears.

I crossed my fingers and hugged Petey in my arms. I checked my Mickey Mouse watch. It was 10:35 AM when Wilbur released the restraining wire and held the wing up as he raced along with the Flyer, heading down the track on the dune. The sun shone brightly that day on the wings of the Flyer as it flew off the track, cleared the dune, and went airborne. The men and the boy left behind gave a great cheer as it raised into the air and soared, proud as any bird in flight. The man with the camera had snapped a picture, the picture I'm sure I had seen in the museum.

Suddenly the wings went into a wobble and the plane pitched up and down, lowered, and hit the sand. Wilbur stopped the timer. "Only twelve seconds, but it FLEW!" he said. They all ran down to congratulate Orville and carry the Flyer back up the dune.

"John, will you measure the distance for the journal?" Orville asked the cameraman.

When John returned with the measurement he was smiling. "One hundred twenty feet is the official first measurement, Captain Wright, sure as my name is John Daniels," he said. "I can't wait to tell the rest of the beach safe guard crew about the Wright Brothers' success this late fall. They always want an update."

Petey and I watched Orville and Wilbur take turns flying the plane; each time they got more control over the wings and gained distance. I felt so proud of the Wright Brothers. During the fourth flight Wilbur soared in the flyer for almost a full minute–it seemed like an hour of pure, heart-pounding excitement. According to John, the last flight went eight hundred and fifty-two feet.

Petey and I were jumping up and down cheering when it happened–a huge gust of wind caught the Wright Brothers' Flyer and flipped it off the sandy ground. It dragged the plane over the cactus-filled terrain, ripping the cloth-covered wings and breaking the wooden struts between them. It lay there like a poor bird with broken wings. Everyone froze in disbelief.

Finally, Orville clapped his hands and said, "Well, now, wasn't that a piece of rotten luck. I believe we are finished for this season, brother. Now, which of us will send the telegram with the good news to Father? We actually did it, brother–we flew our plane through the air!"

The brothers hugged and pounded each other on the back as the men all continued to shout and cheer. Once more, the scene folded in on itself, and Orville told me to hold on to his shirt-tail so he could guide Petey and me safely back through the rushing air of the dark Time Tunnel.

Petey and I stood back at the Wright Brothers Museum, up at the top of the dune. We both blinked our eyes in the bright sunshine as the glare bounced off the glistening white stone of the monument. I felt unstable, and staggered a few steps in confusion. Had I just imagined all of that business with Orville Wright?

"Excuse me, miss, are you feeling ill?" said a man.

I turned to see the man in the Hawaiian shirt, the one who looked like Orville...or was Orville. I wasn't sure any more.

He gave a smile. *"The Time Tunnel can do that to you, the dizziness and all. You'll get used to it."*

I took a deep breath of the salty, fresh air. "Oh, Mr. Orville, I don't know that I want to do this...whatever strange thing it is. Thank you for showing me your boyhood home, and I'll never forget being there with you and your brother to see your first flight. It was...amazing."

"I don't think you have a choice about your special gifts. They're already within you, ready to bloom. You have a mission and a mystery to solve, but I can help you through this first, new responsibility, if you like," Orville said.

I took another shaky breath and nodded my thanks. I reached into my pocket for the bandana to wipe my sweaty face. Petey whined a bit and put his paws up on my leg.

"Jinx, you need some water and some shade. Me, too," Petey said.

"Your Petey is correct. I've kept you too long in the bright sunshine. I'll leave you for now with a last message," said Orville. *"Child, do not forget us–your ancestors and the other pioneers. We were real people. We had families, dreams, and big jobs to do. We were wonderers, thinkers, discoverers, and inventors. We worked hard to forge a new and better life for our children and grandchildren. Do not take us for granted, and please, do not forget us."*

Having delivered his message, he walked away and faded from my view. I gazed at the red handkerchief still in my hand.

"Congratulations on your first flights," I whispered to Orville, but he was gone.

The whole spell broke. Excited voices drifted up to me as tourists with children left their cars in the parking lot and headed towards the museum. Small figures with sunburned faces, bright shirts, and cotton shorts meandered about like an army of colorful ants. Kids called to their brothers, sisters, and friends.

"Come on! Hurry it up, I want to go to the beach," cried one bored-sounding boy to his younger sister.

They had no clue about what I had just witnessed and the importance of it. I wanted to shake them and make them understand. Instead, I started walking down the dunes, deep in thought, with Petey by my side. He poked my leg with his cold, wet nose and looked into my eyes with worry.

"It's Ok, Petey. I think I just had my first real connection with the past. Let's go find Mom. Time to move on."

Petey stayed by my side all the way back to the visitors center.

Chapter Five:

Strange Goings On

Mom made a stop along the trail for us to visit Jockey's Ridge State Park. Talk about big sand dunes. This was another dune as high as Mount Everest to climb with good old speedy Petey.

As we pulled into the rest stop at the park we could see dozens of rainbow colored kites with bow tails flapping in the wind. At one end, brave souls leaped with abandon off the high ridge, strapped onto beautiful hang gliders. The gliders had wingspans of at least thirty feet. They looked like multi-colored pterodactyls floating through the air.

The pilots took off on silent and beautiful flights, weaving their gliders back and forth in the azure sky until the air released them safely back to the ground. I knew why Orville and his brother had journeyed back to the Outer Banks every year to design and test their ideas. The constant seashore breezes provided the perfect uplift needed for flying.

Petey, my adventure dog, wanted us to strap into a bright red and yellow glider and take a leap.

"Super Dog to the rescue!" he said excitedly to me.

"No way, Dude!"

I tried to talk him out of that crazy scheme with a bribe of treats back in the car. Somehow, I don't think our flight would be the silent wonder that everyone else experienced, because I'd be screaming my head off.

"Jinx, let's try it," Mom said.

I stared at her, my mouth open. "Mom, you're not serious," I said.

"Oh, come on, where's your sense of adventure. Dad won't believe us if we actually hang glide. You'll feel like one of the Wright Brothers," said Mom.

If she only knew...I watched some more people strap in and get ready to lift off the dune. Petey started badgering again.

"I know what we should do," I said brightly. "Mom, you tell me these are teachable moments, but I haven't even explored the area yet. Petey, we need to hike around and learn about Jockey's Ridge. We need to learn about the animals and plants, right?" *Good stalling tactic, heh, heh,"* I thought.

"Good stalling tactic, Jinx," my mom said.

I looked sharply at her. "Mom, are you able to read my mind, like everyone else seems to be able to do lately?" I asked.

Mom laughed at my pouty face. "You're so transparent, oh daughter of mine. I don't have to go far to read your mind. Okay, let's explore. Then I'm taking a hang gliding lesson, and you can watch or join in."

Phew. At least I bought me some time. I looked at the gliders soaring in the sun. It did look peaceful and made me feel a connection to Orville, my new friend.

We started on the boardwalk hike up through the dunes. They were beautiful and bright in the sun's glare. Small signs posted here and there told about the wildlife and plant life. I read some of them to Petey.

No wonder this dune looked incredibly high. I read that Jockey's Ridge is the highest dune in the Eastern United States. The Outer Banks islands seem to have all kinds of records: first flight, highest dune. I felt a strange pull to the area, like maybe I had lived here in another lifetime. *Now where did that wild thought come from?*

"Mom, listen to this, 'Jockey's Ridge has three main areas, the Dunes, the Maritime Thicket, and the Roanoke Sound Estuary. This sand was made of quartz from mountain rock millions of years ago. It would take six million dump truck loads of sand to replace the dune.' So cool!

"'The thicket has live oaks, bayberry, sweet gum, red oaks and persimmons.' Uh- oh, Petey, watch out for the animals: red foxes and raccoons and rabbits. No chasing." We looked around, but the animals stayed hidden in the thicket.

I read on. "'The Roanoke Sound Estuary has cattails, and all kinds of sea grasses, like saw grass and giant cord grass. Fish nurseries lie in the sound, and the famous Blue Crabs live there.' Oh, my, gosh! Look at it all..."

We had reached the top of the dune and could see all three parts of the Jockey's Ridge Area. It took my breath away. I felt like I was in the Sahara Desert on top of this massive dune, but when I looked far out on one side I could see the ocean waves rolling in to the beach, and on the other side I saw the quieter waters of the sound.

I also saw the hang gliders. Now they reminded me of brightly colored butterflies, dipping and weaving, bobbing and twisting, all moving with no sound. We stood in complete silence. All I could hear was the faint sound of the surf and the wind rushing by my ears. It was late in the afternoon, so most people had gone to the beaches. My whole body and mind yearned to be up there with the gliders, feeling free of the earth.

"Okay, Mom, let's go gliding," I said. I turned and headed back down the dune boardwalk. Mom smiled, and she and Petey hurried after me.

We signed up at the gift shop and walked out to meet John and Kristin, both college students, who were assigned to us.

"Hello Mrs. MacKenzie, Jinx," John said. "This is my friend, Kristin. Welcome to hang-gliding school." He gave us a lop-sided grin. John's face was freckled and his hair was sandy brown. He wore sneakers, surfer shorts, and a gray tee shirt. "You can feel at ease, because we're both certified Advanced Tandem Instructors with the *United States Hang Gliding Association (USHGA)*."

Kristin was a pretty girl, almost as tall as John. Her hair was dark brown and cut in a style similar to my shaggy red hair. She wore khaki shorts and a bright yellow shirt.

"John and I come here to the Outer Banks every summer to work at the Jockey's Ridge Hang Gliding School," Kristin said. "You're going to love your flight. But the first thing we do before every flight is a safety check of the glider and all of the harness and wires." She demonstrated by showing us the parts of the glider.

"Right," John said. Now for the basics–you'll be flying in tandem with one of us. That means you'll be lying in harness, kind of like a cocoon, over top of the instructor, while we fly the glider."

He showed us our harness and how to fit into it. The harness looked secure and made me feel a lot better about the flight.

"How do you get us up in the air?" I asked.

Kristin picked up the speech again. "It's not hard at all. To launch, we first walk a few steps, then jog, then go into a full run while tilting the glider just right to let the winds pick it up. Once airborne, we'll swing our feet back into this sac, hold the metal bars, and used body position and hand control to guide the glider left and right, and up and down."

"Ready to try it, Jinx?" Mom said. I could tell she worried about whether I really wanted to try hang-gliding.

I felt assured that Kristin and John were safe fliers. I nodded and gave Mom a big grin. "I'm ready, Mom. This will be great!"

We put on helmets and elbow pads and kneepads and got ready to fly. Petey rolled on his back and kicked his legs when he heard he could be strapped in with me. They even had a small helmet for him to wear. Mom and Rick had a purple glider, and guess what–Petey and I got his red and yellow glider. I couldn't believe I was actually going to go on this hang gliding adventure.

Kristin helped me prepare for our flight. "I was about your age when my mom and dad first brought me here to Jockey's Ridge," she said. "I loved the colorful sight of the kites and the hang gliders. I knew I wanted to try it, but when my instructor and took off on my first flight, I about had heart failure. I shut my eyes and didn't open them until we touched down on the sand. I missed my whole first ride," she said. I laughed with her. I knew she was trying to make me feel relaxed, and it worked.

Petey was squirming and kicking. "Petey, stop wiggling," I told him.

"Can't wait, can't wait, can't wait to be in the air. I always wanted to fly like the birds," he said. His short legs were running in the air.

I hugged him tighter. *Animals really have the same dreams we do,* I thought.

We watched Mom and Rick take off from the dune first. It looked so simple–one minute they were standing on the sand, and the next they were soaring.

I took a deep breath as Kristin looked over her shoulder and said, "Ready?"

I nodded. She began to walk, started a jog, and then flat out ran, right off the dune. I don't think she even ran four steps before the wind grabbed us and up, up we were swept, out into the air over the big dune.

"Pppfffffff..." I let out my breath and took another big one. I was exhilarated. This was magical–I was flying. I finally knew what it felt like to be a bird, soaring high in the air. I felt a great kinship with Orville and wondered if he could see me flying. Kristin turned us gently so we flew out over the ocean, back over the dune, up higher, then down and out over the sound side. So quiet, until...

"Wheeeeeeeeee! Wheeeeeeeeee! Wheeeeee!"

It was Petey. He sounded like the little piggy saying wee, wee, wee, all the way home. I didn't know a dog could make that sound. I laughed with pure joy and buried my face in his furry neck. Petey twisted his face back to give me a big kiss.

The flight ended way too soon. I felt Kristin start to guide us down, back in toward the dune. As we got closer to landing, she slipped her feet out of her sac. She pushed the nose of our glider gently up so the air would drag back on the glider and slow us even more. Her feet touched down, and she jogged to a stop. Helpers came to unbuckle Petey and me. I felt so sorry my flight was over. I couldn't wait to tell Max about it. I wondered if he would stop there with his family.

Mom was down, too. She and Rick ran over, and everyone shook hands and patted shoulders, congratulations going all around.

"Mom, that was the best! Aren't you glad I suggested we give it a try?" I teased her.

"Uh, WHO suggested we try hang gliding?" Mom teased right back. Petey bounced up into my arms. I gave Kristin a hug full of wiggling dog.

"You were the perfect tandem partner, Jinx. Come back soon, and be sure to ask for me," Kristen said.

We stopped at the gift shop on the way out, and I bought a tee shirt that had a "Fly Like a Girl" logo. I put hang gliding definitely on my official "Things I Have to Accomplish" list. I'd love to learn how to solo fly.

As our Jeep drove out of the parking lot, I turned and watched the gliders until they were out of sight, then settled in the back seat and chewed on my bottom lip while I considered the day. As much as I had enjoyed the experience, I have to admit my head was still full of thoughts of troubling new powers, Orville Wright, and a mystery yet to be given to me.

After Jockey's Ridge, we drove on through Nags Head to Whalebone, where the road crossed a bridge over the backwaters to Roanoke Island. The view of Roanoke Island from the bridge took my breath away. The sparkling turquoise water of the sound, the flat marshy coastal line, the green woods, the blue sky; those vivid colors filled my senses. I rolled the window down to sniff the beach air. Petey and I stuck our heads way out of the window to try to absorb more of the magical atmosphere into our bodies. My hair and his ears flapped in the air.

We drove to the small village of Manteo, with its colorful shops, stores, and cottages. Summer tourists milled in and out of the gift shops at a snail's pace. I could see lots of shopping in my future.

I felt relaxed and drowsy in the warm, late afternoon sun that shone in on our jeep seats. I wanted to get to our summer home, unpack and relax. Maybe this evening we would go looking for clamshells along the beach.

In the next instant, I noticed the humming of the jeep tires became intense and loud. It sounded like a giant swarm of angry hornets attacking. The bright sun began to fade. I felt dizzy and disoriented. *Oh no, not again.* I reached in my pocket for Orville's silk bandana. I wanted him to help me like he had promised.

Then I felt Orville's presence. "I've something you must see," he said to me. I looked into his dark eyes and shared my fear.

"Why? Why am I being bothered with this...this...scary stuff? I just want to be my regular self...I don't want any of these new powers. I don't want to go into that cold Time Tunnel. What if we get lost?"

Orville sighed, as if dealing with a stubborn child. "Why? Because you are quite capable of handling the situation. Remember, the powers were always part of your "regular self," as you called it. They lay dormant, waiting until you became old enough to use them. You won't be alone. I'll be watching over you, and your new friend, Max, will help you. And you'll always have Petey," Orville said. "He will help and protect you. He is a very special dog, your angel dog." Orville stooped to gently stroke Petey. "Now, hold on to my shirttail."

I reached out and grabbed Orville's shirttail. I squinted my eyes closed until my head ached. Cold, rushing, swirling; there we went again, off into the Time Tunnel of my fears.

I thumped to the ground, and I knew we had to be back in time. No more shops and people rushing into them for souvenirs. My view of Roanoke Island darkened slowly until all I could see was deep, shadowed woodland. It was so real that I heard the buzz of pesky mosquitoes and gnats and felt the steamy shore humidity of the forest pressing in on me. Warblers and thrushes sang to each other. Small furry muskrats and marsh rabbits scuttled in under the shrub thickets. A gray fox slipped by, rustling the leaves, in search of food for her kits. Petey quivered with energy, but he stayed by my side.

SNAP! The large sound filled the air, as loud as the crack of a whip. In the sudden silence, all the creatures seemed to be whisked away by witchy fingers. Someone had stepped on a branch.

I was the watcher of another watcher. The huddled shape of a Native American crouched behind a large old cedar tree. He looked magnificent, clothed in breechcloth and a headband with a few smoke colored feathers tucked in. A knife hung from his shell-beaded belt. His tanned arms and hands touched the rough bark of the tree for support.

The Indian froze in silence. Nothing moved but his crow-black eyes as they tracked something through the woods. It was not he who had disturbed the peace.

My eyes shifted, scanning the silent woods, frantic to search for a clue as to what he was watching. Off to the left, two scurrying shapes whispered in agitation. A colonial lady, dressed in a long skirt, black stockings, and black-laced boots, tugged impatiently as she grasped the arm of a smaller person. A little girl about three or four years old stumbled along behind her. She had beautiful, long brown hair braided in a neat plait and tied at the bottom with a pink ribbon. Her pink dress stopped short of her tiny feet. She wore miniature, laced-up boots similar to those worn by the woman.

The little girl gestured, and I could tell she wanted to go back. The woman stopped, sank to her knees, and placed her hands on the little girl's shoulders. Her eyes surveyed the entire area around them, looking for danger before she whispered to the child. Finally the little girl hung her head and stopped pulling. The woman stood, checked the shadowy forest again, and they joined hands and hurried once more along the trail.

What is this, I thought. What am I seeing? I felt their fear as if it were my own. Where were they going? What was wrong? I also felt the little girl's sadness and disappointment. I knew... she longed for a treasured item now lost to her. I yearned to help the girl.

Petey's cold tongue licked the salty tears from my face and jolted me back into reality. Mom glanced in the rear view mirror and noticed my tears. She pulled the jeep over to the side of the sandy road.

"Jinx, what's wrong? I thought you were asleep back there. You've been so quiet and thoughtful since we left Jockey's Ridge."

I shook my head, partly to clear the cobwebs out of my brain, and partly because I really did not know what was wrong. The lingering sense of sadness faded quickly. Had Orville just taken me to the past, again? Or is this whole thing a bunch of dreams?

"I don't know, Mom," I told her, "I had a sad dream."

I knew what I witnessed had been real to me, but my addled brain couldn't make any sense out of it. I must have been hallucinating. Why were these spooky things happening to me out of the blue? I understood my weird talent of animal communication and feel comfortable with that ability. But this...seeing people right out of the past, hearing messages, and experiencing their lives right there with them...? This was beyond anything I had ever known.

Mom jumped out of the jeep, came around to my side, and opened my door. She knelt down and put her hands on my shoulders, just like the colonial lady had done to the little girl.

"Jinx, is there anything you would like to tell me?"

I shook my head slowly. "Sometime, Mom. But not right now." I needed time to think.

Mom looked at me for a long moment, then smiled gently, got up, and moved back to her seat. She gazed into the mirror, buckled up, and started the engine.

"We've all had a long, exciting day of it," Mom said. "Let's get to the cottage and relax before we haul in the bags and unpack. I feel like having hamburgers and salad tonight. Petey, what do you say we get our food bowls moved in for the summer? It's high time."

Mom was cool like that. She respected my wishes, knowing that I would talk to her when I felt the time right. Petey raised one brown and white paw and touched my face.

"Jinx, you will help, and everything will be good," he told me.

Then he gave me a big kiss with his pink tongue and jumped up to the front seat beside Mom. Petey rode shotgun, determined to get us to our final destination without any more delay.

Chapter Six:

Midnight Visitor

I decided to put the eerie happenings of the day in the back of my mind to think about some other time. I was too tired, and ready for a mental break. Petey's delight at being released to explore our cottage and yard perked me right up. He leaped out of the red jeep and hit the ground running. Petey ran onto the small front porch to the door and jumped up and down on all four legs, trying to see into the cottage. He looked like a coiled jack-in-the box going up, down, up, down–boing, boing. Then he tore off down the sandy path that led to the rear of the cottage.

"I like our cottage. We can put my outside bed on the back porch. Water bowl, too. See what's out back? Gulls! Bark, bark, bark," said Petey.

His excitement was contagious. I chased after him to check it out for myself. Running felt wonderful after our long road trip.

Weathered shingles and gingerbread trim covered the outside of our cottage. It was painted pale yellow, with faded blue trim around the windows, doors, and porch rails. The two-story bungalow had a front porch and a rear screened-in porch. Comfortable-looking wicker sofas and chairs with flowered cushions sat on the porches, and a porch swing swayed in the slight breeze.

Collections of twisted and polished driftwood, and pink, tan, and yellow shells of all sizes decorated the wicker tables and lay on the floor along the sides of the porches. Shiny whelk shells formed tidy borders for flower gardens filled with purple and yellow coneflowers and zinnias.

Sandy soil and beach grasses filled the yard, which led the way to rounded dunes covered in sea oats and eelgrass. Yaupon holly, full of green, waxy berries, grew among the grasses. Mom told me the berries would turn bright red by late summer and offer a delicious treat for the birds.

The dunes rolled right down to the lapping sound water. A few cottages could be seen here and there through the dune grasses. A teen-age boy and girl walked along our beach, gathering shells. A lady relaxed in a striped beach chair near the water's edge.

It was so peaceful and quiet. I heard only the gentle lapping of the waters and soft calls of the shore birds. The sun neared the horizon and backlit the clouds in purples, oranges, and glorious reds.

I sank down in the sand, kicked off my sneakers, and grabbed my knees up to my chest. A grin split my face from ear to ear. I felt the calm and quiet surround me. Petey galloped up and sprawled in my lap, finally winded and ready to snuggle. I stroked his silky ears.

I heard Mom softly kicking sand as she walked barefoot, swinging her sandals at her side. She dropped down beside me, shoulder to shoulder, stretched out her long legs, and leaned back on her elbows. Together we watched the colorful sunset.

"How do you like the place, Jinx?" she asked quietly.

"I love it so much already that I think my heart is breaking. Mom, I know I started out with a bad attitude today. But along the way some things happened that really have me thinking about the past in a different way. I've been having some...strange dreams, too."

"Hallelujah, praise be!" Mom shouted, throwing her arms in the air.

"Don't tease me. I mean it, Mom. I still can't completely understand it, but I feel different. I feel like I have a job to do here, something besides writing a good paper for my history teacher, that is."

I gave her a sideways grin, and she grinned back. She reached over and ruffled my hair, then Petey's ears.

"I think you have big things to do this summer, young lady. Now, let's go see the inside of our little home away from home."

We got up, brushed the sand from our backsides, and followed Petey back up the dune path to our yellow and blue cottage.

Our cottage was just as wonderful inside as it was outside. The living room had a sofa and two chairs that you could just melt into. Little end tables and footstools sat by the sofa, and lots of bright pictures hung on the walls. The cottage was decorated in a seashore theme, from the fabric on the furniture to the knick-knacks on the walls and tables. The honey-colored hardwood floors had braided rag rugs. Sea-foam green walls made the room cool and inviting.

As we lugged boxes and bags of groceries into the kitchen area, I admired our cozy seashore kitchen. Pale blue curtains framed the bright windows. I threw open the windows and the curtains started blowing in the evening breeze. Ah, that tangy, beachy smell teased the senses.

We unpacked the food in a hurry and put it into the yellow cupboards. A black potbelly stove sat in the corner, next to cushioned window seats. The oak table and chairs looked like a great place to have our meals while we discussed our daily plans.

We chatted and laughed as Mom grilled some burgers, and I made a fresh garden salad. Petey pulled his toy bag, bed, and bowls into the kitchen and arranged them beside the potbelly stove. I gave him some fresh water and filled his dish with chow. What a happy guy.

After we checked out the rest of the house, Mom claimed the downstairs bedroom with the old oak bed. Pale blue walls and wooden chests made her room look cozy and cool.

The loft area upstairs would be my bedroom. Petey and I dragged my gear up the wooden hill to check out our summer nest. I grinned with pure pleasure because it was so beautiful. It had a big brass bed covered with a patchwork quilt. Tucked in under the slanted roof, my room offered an outside balcony porch with another swing.

Petey jumped onto the bed and rolled over on his back, kicking his furry legs in happiness.

"Nice room, Jinx. We'll have so much fun this summer."

"I feel really happy too, Pete-o. Now let's go have the brownies and milk Mom promised after we finished unpacking. Then I'm ready to hit the hay."

"Max coming soon?"

"Yeah, he's due in tomorrow. I can't wait."

"Good, Jinx needs a helper."

Helper? To do what? Petey knew something that I didn't. I felt a little uneasy when I stopped on one of the steps and looked at Petey's furry face. But he just grinned his silly doggie grin and ran for the kitchen. I ran after him.

Some small sound awakened me. I felt disoriented and quickly reached out to touch Petey's soft back for comfort. He wasn't there. In the pale moonlight coming through my open windows, I could see him in the middle of the room with his head cocked and on the alert. He stared toward the direction of our balcony.

My heart thudded against my ribs so hard I thought for sure Mom must be able to hear it down below. I could tell it was way after midnight. What had awakened me? Petey took a few steps, and then he laid his ears back against his head. I wondered where I had put Orville's bandana. I grabbed it from my nightstand. It was then I realized I'd come to rely on it for comfort.

"Petey, what's wrong?"

"Grrrrrrrr..."

"You're scaring me, Fur Face."

I looked over at the screen doors to the balcony. A frigid air seemed to penetrate the room. What was going on? A misty fog filtered in through the screen. I grabbed my covers and dived underneath.

Great–just stinking great. All I needed to round out a perfectly strange day was to dream about a ghost. I pinched my arm hard and gave out a little yelp. Ouch, I was awake all right. I peeked out from under the edge of my quilt, and there stood a small misty form just inside the door that led to the balcony. Petey stopped growling and began wagging his tail. Oh, good, Petey makes friends with the ghost, I thought. Now what, I invite her for a sleepover?

I took a deep breath and sat straight up in bed, still grasping my covers around my neck for comfort. The moonlight helped me to see a bit better as Petey took a few more steps, wagging his tail. The mist solidified into the figure of a little girl in a long, pink dress.

I knew instantly it was the little girl I had seen in the vision earlier today. She reached out her arms to me, as if she wanted to tell me something. Then she pointed behind her and beckoned me to come with her.

"Yeah, right," I yelped out loud, as I dove once more for the safety of my blankets. I whipped them back over my head and frantically whispered to Petey.

"P-P-Pe-Petey! Tell me this isn't happening. Get over here and protect me."

"She's a nice girl, Jinx. She needs our help."

"Fur Face, I draw the line. N-O, no." Where was Orville when I needed him?

Thump. Something landed on the bed with me. The girl ghost was attacking me? This time I screamed out loud. It tried to pull the covers off me. I thrashed around like a harpooned whale, kicking at my covers until I fell with an undignified jolt to the floor.

There sat my furry buddy, licking my face. I could swear he was laughing. The room warmed once more. I glanced at the balcony door, but I could already tell my post-midnight visitor was gone. Some small child had reached out to me from the past. Now there was no doubt about it. Mom was right. I did have big things to do this summer, and I didn't think I had any choice in the matter.

Chapter Seven:

Max's Side Trip

Max felt odd. He couldn't quite put his finger on it, but he kept thinking he was on the verge of something new and big this summer. At certain times he tingled all over, sort of like a cold breeze had touched him. It started last winter at school.

Then there were the dreams–they hit more often now–a couple times a week. He dreamed about the past, wars and fights, Indians and soldiers, troubling things. They were vivid, colorful events that felt like he was right there, watching amidst the action.

When he talked to his dad about them, his dad said it was growing pains. He advised Max not to read his favorite historical books right before he went to sleep. But Max noticed his dad gave him strange, worried looks every now and then.

When he met Jinx, the odd feelings washed over him again, stronger than ever. She *was* very cute, but the attraction was definitely more than that. He *knew* this girl and he were meant to be friends for a bigger purpose.

Tonight Max was so restless he couldn't sleep. His body felt wired, and it hummed with electricity. He had enjoyed the day at the Wright Brothers Museum and his hang gliding experience off the top of Jockey's Ridge. He should be well into an exhausted sleep by now. But darned if that weird, tingly feeling hadn't dogged him all day. *Sorry Petey,* he thought, smiling.

"That's okay, Max. Can't wait to see you. Can't wait! Yip, Yip!"

Whoa, where did that come from? That felt like I received the message directly from Petey, Max thought. *That was a telepathic message.* He sat bolt upright in his bed and actually checked the room to see if somehow Petey had gotten in. Of course, Petey wasn't there. Max lay back down, rubbing his forehead at the beginnings of a headache. That was another part of the new, odd stuff going on–headaches.

Max could hear his dad's soft snores from the open door of the other bedroom in their motel suite. That comforted him. *My dad and mom are the best,* he thought. *But sometimes they hover over me like a helicopter. They need to back off, just a little bit.* Max resembled his dad, sharing the blond hair and blue eyes of the family. His mom had soft, brown eyes and coal black hair.

He turned onto his stomach and pounded his fists into the pillows to fluff them up, determined to go to sleep. *Please let me sleep,* Max thought. *I don't want to dream I'm someone from the past. I don't want to be anyone but me.* He willed his brain to slow down and relax and took deep, relaxing breaths. *I'll think about Jinx and Petey. I'll have to teach her to surf...*

Finally Max slipped into a deep sleep that took him into another amazing, frightening dreamscape. *What am I doing on this beach? Who's that guy there...the one with the paper and quill pens...whoa... stop! It feels like I'm sliding right into his mind...stop!*

Summer, 1585–On the Beach of Roanoke Island
Two Years Before the Colonists Arrive

John White, master artist for the Queen, filled in the details of his sketches as fast as his memory allowed. He sat on the warm beach of Roanoke Island in the early morning light, with sleeves rolled up, shaded only by his broad-brimmed hat.

White paused from his sketches and lifted his eyes to the surroundings. Puffy clouds filled a brilliant blue sky, and gulls swooped and glided over-head. The honking of swans and geese drew his attention skyward. Brown pelicans flew by in a long, low line, skimming the waters for schools of tiny silver fish. I must remember to get all of the fowl into my sketches, he thought. This could be a great land to begin a new life. The sound waters lapped gently near his feet.

Sir Richard Grenville was in charge of this 1585 expedition. Sir Walter Raleigh wanted Grenville to pick an area that would be a perfect setting for an English colony, build a fort, and establish a permanent settlement in America.

A few days ago, Manteo, their friendly Croatoan Indian leader, had taken the English explorers across the sound to the mainland. Manteo was newly returned from a trip to England to meet the Queen.

Sir Richard had ridden in the lead boat with his gentleman advisors. Fifty troops led by Ralph Lane had filled the other three boats in the flotilla. They were outfitted with food and supplies for eight days.

Manteo had introduced them to three Indian villages. The natives had proudly guided the Englishmen through their villages. They traded fruits and vegetables and wild game meat and smoked fish for English trinkets. The gold and silver buttons on the white men's clothing and the shiny swords by their sides especially fascinated them.

White went back to his sketches. He wanted to show what an organized, intelligent group of people already lived here in America. He finished drawing the circular stockade of high poles around the one small village they had visited. Eighteen structures stood within this village. The largest appeared to be their temple–a sacred place of worship. It was rounded and covered with skins. The other structures were built rectangular in shape. Some buildings were closed in and covered with skins, while others were open-ended.

Another village had straight streets and paths throughout, with similar housing for the villagers. Fields of maize, beans, peas, and gourds lay in front of the village with woods to the rear. White had drawn the Indians hunting deer in the forest. They hunted with bows as tall as a man and sharp arrows crafted to fly straight to their target.

Next, he carefully worked on the sketch showing how they fished. It was a quite simple, but brilliant plan, he thought. The natives implanted a wall of sturdy poles across an area of the sound to trap the fish within the boundaries of the fence us-

ing nets of woven reeds. They could wade in the shallow water and spear the fish, or paddle in their dugout boats and use their spears.

The making of the boats was in itself fascinating to see. The Indians chopped tall, straight trees to the ground and stripped the branches. Next they hammered and chiseled out one side, setting small fires to burn out the center, scooping out the burnt wood, and continuing to shape and chisel the insides. This was a lengthy process, but their craftsmanship formed beautiful boats in the end.

White had tried to draw a sampling of the varied fish: a catfish, a burrfish, a skate in a trap, sturgeon, a hammerhead shark, and a king crab. He also drew in some land crabs and a loggerhead turtle. What a land of plenty, he thought.

The Indians in this village had held a celebration to welcome the strange white men from far away. Natives from other villages were also invited to the feast. They gathered in a cleared field with a rounded pole in the center. A circle of high poles surrounded the center pole. These poles were quite curious, White thought. Each one had a different, carved face on top.

He paused to remember what he had witnessed at the ceremony. The natives had sent three women to the center pole. They faced inward and hugged each other around the pole. Then men from the different tribes placed themselves in between the outer poles and danced and pranced, chanted and shook dried gourd rattles, until they exhausted themselves. When they left the circle, others took their place. The dancing went on for hours, until they finally broke for the feast.

The feast offered the finest food the new land had to offer. They all dined on roasted venison, duck, and rabbit, smoked fish, roasted corn and a type of corn bread, and turtle soups with peas, beans, and potatoes. Melons, gourds, wild fruit, nuts, sunflower seeds, and berries rounded off the feast of plenty. Sir Richard had talked with excitement of this land with his advisors–surely a successful English colony could be planted here in this fertile land.

White nodded his head in agreement, remembering the spectacular feast. Most of my sketches are ready for my watercolors, White thought. I have much to finish–it should keep me busy on the trip home.

He paged through his pictures, checking over the way he had depicted the Indians. A native man, tall and muscular, wearing little but a small animal skin tied at the waist and covering his front. His head was shaved into a crest running from forehead to back. A woman, also tall and capable, wearing only an apron of skin covering her front, with hair in dark bangs and long curls in the back. Ear piercings of small shells were common on the men, and the women wore strings of beads around their necks. Their limbs were covered in flowery tattoos.

White put his pens down and smiled as he studied the pictures of the women. He remembered another visit they had made to Wingina's village. Wingina's wife had run out to meet the men. She and her helpers invited the leaders into her lodge and bathed them and washed and dried their clothes. They were treated to another feast of tasty food and waited on hand and foot by the happy group of Indian women.

When braves approached bearing their bows and arrows, she ran to them and angrily chattered at the men. The braves laid their weapons on the ground, raised their arms, and backed away. White chuckled to think of how the men listened to her, as she obviously felt it her job to protect these white visitors.

I want to do them justice, he told himself. I want to show those in England what a noble people these natives are–tall and proud, and eager to be friends. Satisfied for now, White closed his sketchbook. He jumped when someone called his name.

"John White, Sir Richard wishes to speak to you," said a soldier. He wore a metal helmet and breastplate, with his long sword swinging at his side. The soldier turned and walked back to a larger group.

White sighed and gathered up his equipment. I know what this is about, he thought. I have a bad feeling. Sir Richard had grumbled and complained ever since they had returned from their exploring expedition. His favorite silver cup that he had taken along on the voyage had gone missing, and Sir Richard wanted it back. He blamed the Indians at the last village they had visited.

"Ah, White, there you are. I want you to accompany a contingency of soldiers back to that blasted Indian village, Aquascococke, where someone stole my silver cup. I shall have it back, or they shall suffer the consequences," said Grenville.

"Sir Richard, I am afraid you are making a bad mistake," said White. "We can't be sure where the cup was lost. Perhaps it fell overboard, or someone within our own group... er...borrowed it. The Indians are friendly and peaceful. This could stir up problems and break the peace. It could endanger further dealings with the natives and cause problems for future English settlements. We must try by all means to maintain friendly relations."

"Ha! There's only one way to deal with people like that. It's no different than training a dog," Sir Richard snapped his fingers. "I'll teach them who will rule this land. We're not to be trifled with."

It was obvious to John White that the soldiers were no more comfortable with the idea of raiding the Indian village than he was. Regardless of their feelings about the matter, they were trained soldiers in the Queen's service, and they would follow their superiors' orders, but they shifted their weight from side-to-side and threw furtive sidelong glances at each other behind the nobleman's back. And if any of them knew anything about the whereabouts of the cup, no one mentioned it.

"I want your observations of the situation and to have you report back to me," Sir Richard continued. "Manteo will go along as interpreter. The boat is ready to leave."

White left his artist's supplies and drawings in a basket at the campsite, and he followed the chosen soldiers and Ralph Lane, their commander, to the boats.

A few days' journey brought them back to Aquascococke. As they marched to the village, the heavy tramping of the armored men drowned out the call of the birds and sent the wildlife scurrying deep into the wooded land. No one spoke. The troops had to wipe the sweat from their faces and swat away the insects constantly. They were dressed in full armor and carried swords and muskets. Some of the men had heavy packs on their backs. White wondered if the packs all contained supplies or some other hidden items.

Children ran to great them, remembering the excitement of having the strange men visit their village. They weren't afraid a bit and marched alongside the troops. Lane marched right into the village, where the village elders greeted them.

"Go on then, Manteo. Tell them Sir Richard Grenville's silver cup is missing. Tell them it must be somewhere in this village, and they must give it back," said Lane.

Manteo asked about the missing silver cup. He had an animated discussion with the chief of the village, hands and fingers moved along with the words. White could tell things were not going well by watching the faces of the head tribesmen and the villagers. Frowns and fear replaced smiles on their faces.

White watched as the chief turned to his people and spoke in a loud voice. Mouths dropped open. They appeared to be shocked as they looked all around at each other. Heads began to shake, and a few young men questioned their chief, waving their arms and pointing to the soldiers. Angry voices started to shout out, but their chief quieted them with a wave of his arm. He turned back to Manteo and crossed his arms. The chief spoke briefly.

Manteo turned to Ralph Lane and talked in short clips of English that he had learned over the past year spent among the white men.

"The chief says they do not have the silver cup. He asked his people. They say the white chief packed it in his bag. They do not have it," Manteo repeated.

"Tell them someone is not telling the truth. They better search the village and return the cup, or there will be punishment," said Lane.

Manteo frowned but turned back to the village chief. He delivered Lane's words. The chief spoke only one brief phrase. Manteo looked at Lane.

"He says they do not have the silver cup. His people speak the truth."

Lane became furious. "We will retreat to the lake and camp for the rest of the day. They have until sundown to return the cup. Tell them, Manteo." He shouted orders at the troops, and they turned on their heels and marched out of the village.

Lane marched the men to the lakeside beach and had them break down to wait. They built campfires and prepared some food. Some of the men began guard duty. Soldiers not on guard duties still watched the surrounding woods while they sat and talked in low tones. John White went to speak with Lane.

"The Indians denied having the silver cup. How can they produce something they do not have, Ralph Lane?" he asked.

"They are lying," said Lane. "I have strict orders to return with the silver cup, or take care of the problem."

"What do you mean, take care of the problem?" White said.

Lane shrugged. "Military orders are on a 'need to know' basis, and you have no need to know," he said. "You may return to your campfire and wait."

John White looked at the large, mysterious packs lying in a pile as he returned to his log to wait. Again, a dreadful feeling washed over him. This cannot end well, he thought.

Later, as the sun lowered over the lake in beautiful shades of red and violet, no one from the Indian village had approached their temporary campsite to return the silver cup. The men were restless and even more alert as they darted looks toward their leader, awaiting orders. The camp became so silent that the night insects' and lake toads' and katydids' loud chirping and croaking took over.

Darkness and hordes of mosquitoes descended upon the campsite. Lane called the men to attention. "It seems the natives refuse to be honest and return the cup. We will go ahead with retaliation. Open the packs containing the clubs and torches. Every soldier will carry a lighted torch. We want them to see us coming. I want every planted field and every building set afire. Burn them to the ground. If the Indians interfere, hit them with your clubs and swords. If necessary, shoot them. Those are Sir Richard's orders. Now, let's move out."

"Please reconsider, Lane. This is not fair to the Indians," White shouted. But Lane totally dismissed him without a word.

John White felt sick to his stomach. The natives had been nothing but trusting, friendly, and open with his group. They had traded fairly and treated the white men with respect, offering them feasts and entertainment. Now this is how Grenville's group repays them? White jumped up to follow the group of marching soldiers.

The villagers had settled into their homes for the night. Confusion and panic broke out when the frightful-looking troops entered their village carrying lit torches. Men, women, and children poured out of their homes when they were set on fire. Yelling, screaming, crying, frustration, and anger filled the air.

The natives fled through the thick smoke into the forest to get away from the fires that soon raged through the village. Musket shots rang out as nervous soldiers fired off their weapons. The flickering flames raged high into the air, lighting the Indians' tortured faces and casting soot and ash over everyone. The fields of maize, the corn that they depended upon for winter food and bread, all burned to the ground. The hungry flames ate up the homes, tools, and hunting weapons, and other buildings they had built with pride.

The soldiers finally stood at attention, silent and grim as they watched everything disappear in the angry fires. Lane kept them on watch until the dim light of dawn appeared in the east–when all that was left of the village was a smoking pile of burnt ashes. Then he ordered the men into ranks and marched them back to their boats.

"*Ahhhhhhhh...*" Max kicked off his covers and ran, banging into a wall. He grabbed a blanket and swatted at the floor as he tried to put out the fire in his dream. His dad and mom came into Max's room to see what on earth was going on. They grabbed Max and shook him to try and get his attention.

"Max, stop it, wake up–you're safe, it's okay," his dad said, as he wrapped his arms around his struggling son.

Max was covered in sweat, and his breath heaved in and out, but he finally realized he was safe in his dad's arms.

"Oh, Dad, Mom, I had the worst dream. But I don't think it was a dream–I think it was real. I was this man named John White, and I was on an exploration of this area, way back in history. And the Indians were kind and friendly and they showed the Englishmen their villages and crops and had a feast and everything, but then some other rich guy...I forget his name, but he was in charge, he lost his stupid silver cup and blamed it on the Indians, and he ordered the soldiers to go back to their village and get it from them, but...but they said they didn't have it, so the English soldiers set their fields and houses on fire and...and it was awful–the flames were sky high..."

"Whoa, slow down, son," said Max's dad. He led his son back to his bed and sat him down.

His mom came out of the bathroom with a cool, wet washcloth for her son's forehead. She gently wiped his face and talked in soothing tones.

"There you go, Max. That's right, settle down, it was just a nightmare," Mom said. She gave her husband a worried look, and he pressed his lips into a tight line and gave a slight nod.

Max's heartbeat slowed down as he listened to his mom's calming words. He closed his eyes and blew out a big breath of air. Then he opened his eyes and stared into his dad's blue eyes. "It wasn't a nightmare, it was real. I could hear and see everything John White did, like I was him." Max blinked his own blue eyes as he carefully watched his dad. His dad nodded.

"I *understand*, Max. Do you know who John White was?" asked Dad.

"Not really. Not before the dream or vision or whatever it was. But now I know he was an artist for the Queen. Back when the explorers came to America. Only the Native Americans already lived here. It started early on, didn't it? Us mistreating the Indians?"

Dad nodded again. "You'll have to do some research on this. It'll help you understand your...um...dreams. I guess coming to the Outer Banks has triggered something for you." Dad glanced at Max's mother again.

"Okay, men, we better get back to sleep if we want any energy to move in to our cottage, tomorrow," Max's mother said. She held the covers up for Max to scoot back into bed, and then covered him and gave his forehead a light kiss. "I love you, Max."

"Yeah, I love you, too, big guy," Max's dad said.

Max grinned at them. "I know. Me too."

"We'll hold you to that in a year or two, when you think we're the dumbest people on the planet earth," Mom said. Max laughed out loud.

His parents waited until they could hear Max settle into sleep before they got back to bed.

"Ward, you know you're going to have to tell Max sometime soon," Mom whispered.

"I know," Dad said. "I hoped it would have skipped Max, but things are starting to get out of control for him, and Max deserves to know what's going on with his own body and his abilities." He sighed.

The curtains were open to the night sky, and the full moon lit the side of the room. Max's dad opened his left hand and looked at the burnt grass and ashes he had brushed off of his son's shoulder. He blew them off his hand and brushed away the soot mark they left behind on his palm. The ashes drifted through the air, blown by the currents sent from the air conditioner vent, until they settled on the gray carpet, under the bed.

Chapter Eight:

Connecting Clues

"Jinxxxx! Time to get up, you sleepy head. It's past nine. You're sleeping your day away," Mom called from the kitchen.

When I opened my eyes, the sun shone brightly through the little window above my bed. Petey was already downstairs. I smelled the rich aroma of Mom's coffee brewing and bacon frying.

I jumped out of bed and pulled on my red bathing suit, denim shorts, and a purple tee shirt. Then I ran my fingers through my spiky red hair, grabbed my sneakers, and hopped down the stairs.

I didn't allow myself to think too much about my strange visitor from the past in the middle of the night. Everything felt fine this morning. The bright sunlit day tended to chase away the shadows of the night. The disturbance puzzled me now, rather than frightened me. *So, what's up with all this stuff, anyway? And am I even brave enough to find out? I mean, c'mon! Time travel and ghosts in the night? And Orville wasn't exactly popping up to help me solve these mysteries,* I thought to myself.

"Morning, Mom. Morning, Petey," I called, then washed up in the downstairs bathroom, and joined them in the kitchen.

Petey wagged his stubby tail at me. He had his snoot buried in his morning kibble. He didn't seem to be in the least upset by any of the "Big Mystery" as I had begun to call it.

I poured the orange juice while Mom dished up the scrambled eggs. We sat together at our oak table to enjoy the first official breakfast of our summer vacation. The salty air wafted in through the curtained kitchen windows and mingled with the good breakfast aromas. We felt comfortable and happy as we munched on our buttered toast.

"Mom, did you ever have anything...uh, strange happen to you? You know, like something kind of scary that you couldn't explain?"

Mom looked thoughtful for a moment, then she said, "Yes, I know what you mean, Jinx. I've experienced some pretty strange things in my life. Eventually they tended to explain themselves, or I just tucked them away as life experiences and didn't fret too much about them."

I took a bite of my toast, chewed and swallowed, "Um...would you think I'm crazy if I told you I've seen people from the past, Mom? And that they seem to have messages for me and want me to help them..." I finished in a rush, "and that I just can't figure out how to do that, yet."

I had taken a big risk, but I *had* to talk about it. Mom put down her fork and looked into my eyes with intensity. She seemed to be measuring her words carefully before she answered.

"No, I wouldn't think you are crazy. I'd think you are very talented and have some special gifts. It appears that you are only beginning to use some of these gifts. There is magic in the air everywhere, but only a few of us are really tuned in to it. You are one of those lucky people."

Petey finished his breakfast and came over to sit by the table. He looked back and forth from Mom to me and listened to every word we said.

I wondered about how Mom worded it when she said, 'only a few of *us* are really tuned into it.' *Maybe it runs in the family. How strange.*

Mom, did you...do *you* have this strange gift?" I asked.

Mom gazed out the window, then looked back at me. She nodded her head ever so slightly.

Great, I thought. *I caught this from my mother.* "Well, I don't feel lucky. I'm not sure I want the challenge of helping people from long ago. It's too scary," I said.

"You are definitely your mother's daughter." Mom laughed. "I guess it's time to talk with you more about your gift. You and I are more alike than you could ever imagine. And you're even more like your Aunt Merry."

"Aunt Merry has the gift?"

"There's plenty of time to talk, later. Meanwhile, why don't you take a morning jog over the dunes to Max's cottage, and see if they've arrived. You can help them move in and show Max the beach. I have a good feeling about that boy. I think he'll be a great listener. Maybe he can help you figure it out."

Mom was right. Since Max shared some of my special gifts, he might be the perfect person to talk with about the strange details of the Big Mystery. I wondered if it ran in his family, like it appeared to do so in mine. I grabbed a striped beach towel and a lightweight windbreaker. Petey and I headed out toward Max's cottage.

Max and his parents ran back and forth from the van to the house, carrying bulky bags and suitcases into their front room. They all waved hello to me.

His cottage was as quaint and picturesque as ours. About the same size, it was painted soft green with butter-yellow trim.

Max had on his swim trunks and a cool surfer-dude tee shirt. He gave me a big grin.

"Hey, Jinx, I hoped you'd show up. Help me drag my gear to my room? Then Mom and Dad say I can go swimming. Can't wait to hear if you had any adventures yesterday. Did you see the Wright Brother's Monument and those awesome gliders at Jockey's Ridge?"

He grabbed a lime-green duffle bag and took off at a trot. This boy was more hyperactive than Petey! I sure was glad to see him. We carried his stuff up the stairs to his room, where I collapsed on a stuffed beanbag chair, and he threw his clothes into drawers. Not a real neat freak, I noticed.

He crammed wrinkled, unfolded clothes in and pushed the drawers shut. He stood his boogie boards and surf boards in the corner, dumped a box of books onto some shelves, and threw his empty duffle bag and the boxes into the closet. Shoving the closet door shut with a back kick, he brushed his hands off with a satisfied grunt.

"There. Moved in. Now, let's go catch some rays."

I laughed and shook my head. I wasn't the neatest person in the world but compared to him, Max made me look like tidy and organized.

"What?" he said. "Are you mocking my quick ability of organizing my stuff? Let's roll, Petey. Last one to the beach is a big baboon."

We sounded like a herd of elephants as we stumbled and stomped down the stairs and out to the porch.

"Stick together, you three. And don't forget to use sun block. That sun's hot out there," Max's mother yelled after us. "Come grab some sandwiches when you're hungry...wow... They're off and running. I doubt if they even heard me," she said to Max's Dad.

I stopped and turned back. Max's father looked just like him with his blond hair, blue eyes, and a nice suntan. He wore his hair shaggy and long, and had on blue jeans and a white shirt.

His mom had her black hair cut short with bangs. She was dressed for the beach in a striped coverall and sandals.

"And thanks, Jinx, for helping Max. It's good to see you," said his mom.

"Great to see you, too, Mr. and Mrs. Myers," I said. I gave them a wave, then turned and ran after Max and Petey.

"Max and Jinx are big ba-boons! bark! Bark!" Petey was far ahead of us in a flash.

As those taunting doggie words drifted back to us, I shouted to Max, "Oh yeah, Petey never loses. But let's see who's the bigger baboon, you or me."

We both hit the beach at the same time, laughing. The whole day spread out before us in which to explore, hike and swim. Life was good. The sun shone out of a bright blue sky, and the sound was calm.

We hiked along looking for shells and smooth pebbles, and I told Max about the strange things that happened to me yesterday. I started with the odd meeting of Orville Wright at Kitty Hawk. By the time I got to the part about seeing the colonial woman and the little girl in the woods, he stopped walking and looked at me in amazement. He shielded his eyes from the sun's glare with both hands. It looked like he peered at me through binoculars, like he was inspecting some very strange creature.

I paused, wondering if he thought I was a complete loony bird. Then I pulled Orville's red, silk bandanna out of my pocket and handed it to Max. He fingered it with reverence.

"This is so awesome," he declared. "Jinx, you are like a medium or something. You know–one of those people who have visions about the past and can communicate with people from different time periods. Do you know what a gift you have?"

That's the second time today I heard that one–about having a 'gift.' First it was Mom, now from Max. I continued on with the rest of the whole weird story.

"...and then the girl was gone, like a little wisp of smoke disappearing into the air. It was Petey who jumped on my bed and scared me, not the ghost girl," I finished up. "So what do you think about all this crazy stuff? What should I do next?"

"First of all, don't look so worried. Let's sit down and hash this out."

Max spread out his towel on the sand and grabbed a little journal and a pencil out of his backpack before plopping himself down with a grunt. He started taking notes, his tongue out between his teeth and forehead furrowed.

I was impressed. Max was like a Boy Scout, his room might be messy, but he was prepared for everything. He sounded and looked like a reporter as he started asking me questions.

"Ok, let's see if we can relate any of this stuff. The first weird things that happened were in the Wright Brothers museum with the picture and out on the dunes surrounding their memorial, right? Why do you think Orville appeared to you?"

I chewed on my lip for a moment while I thought about it. "Well... he told me that I had some kind of gift for going back in time and helping people. He said I've always had these powers, and that they've been lying dormant until I was ready to use them. And I definitely remember him saying, "Please don't forget us," at the end, before he left. I know he meant himself and his brother and all of the advancements they accomplished for aviation.

"He made himself so real to me. It's the first time I actually thought of anyone in history as a real person. You know, I got to see Orville and Wilbur as boys, experimenting with how to make a whirligig fly better. They called each other Orv and Will, and their mom and dad seemed so nice.

"And Max, I got to witness their first flight day...that was absolutely awesome. Those days at Kitty Hawk and Kill Devil Hills must have been great fun for them, flying kites and gliders to learn about flight. Can you imagine being the first person to accomplish something that spectacular for your country?"

"Whoa, girl. That's quite a speech from a kid who told me yesterday that she couldn't stand boring old history."

"I know. I'm also impressed with my self-improvement, thank you very much." I grinned.

"What else do you think he meant by, "Don't forget us?" Max asked.

"Max, I have the strangest feeling that he also meant for us to remember...uh, everyone from the past, and not just the famous explorers and inventors. He wants us to think about how everyone helped to shape our country. The regular people, moms, dads, and kids just like us, who were really brave–just living their lives in a new world."

"Uh-huh, I see what you mean. You know, I really never considered people in history in a real way, either. They just seem like make-believe action figures or something like that–like movie characters. I wish I had been with you."

"Well, don't hold your breath, but I think you may be in for some of the same weird stuff happening to you. Orville told me you would help me." I looked sideways at Max. He had his forehead wrinkled in thought, as he slowly nodded his head. I could tell he had something important on his mind.

"I...I've been having some really intense dreams lately, myself," Max said. "One was right before we left for the Outer Banks. It was so real, that I thought I was right there in it. It was about an Indian attack on a fort. And last night I had a whopper of a nightmare about a guy named John White. It felt like I was him, an artist for the Queen of England who painted scenes of the Indians' village life. I travelled with this group of explorers. Then an awful thing happened. I'll...uh... tell you about it soon. It might have something to do with all this mystery stuff. Do you think that I might have some special powers, too? Like you? Maybe we were meant to meet each other this summer. Do you think Orville will help me, too?"

We both stared at each other. Maybe it wasn't fair to be glad Max was going through similar scary things like I was experiencing, but all of a sudden, I didn't feel so alone.

Max was right back on track. He looked at his notes. "Now, think about the next strange thing that happened to you. When you arrived on Roanoke Island, Orville showed you the vision of the Native American hiding behind that tree, and the lady and girl hurrying through the woods, right? Think hard now, what other thoughts pop into your head as you're remembering?"

"I know they were dressed like people did in the 1500s or 1600s–you know...long skirts and those frilly caps. I bet that vision really did take place right here, hundreds of years ago. They were so real. The little girl wanted to go back for something. She kept pulling backward and pointing. But the woman, I think it must have been her mother, told her they couldn't go back. I think they were running away from something that scared them, because they were really hurrying, and the mother kept looking over her shoulder and all around.

"I had a bad feeling when I saw the Indian hidden behind that tree, watching them. Something felt wrong, like maybe he meant them harm? He had war paint all over his body."

Max said, "Don't be scared of the Indian. We're not sure about his intentions–maybe he was just interested in the strange people. We really gave the Native Americans a bad deal when the Europeans came to America to explore and settle."

He finally told me about John White and the soldiers, who torched the Indian village and all their crops over a missing silver cup. "It's no wonder they didn't trust the white men," Max said.

I listened carefully. "*Phew*, you're right, Max. That was a terrible thing to do to the natives. But this Indian looked so big and scary. I never met an Indian up close like that, you know?" I said. *But I had to ask myself why my first reaction to the Indian was negative. He really didn't look angry; rather he looked curious.*

"Okay, let's talk about the little girl that visited you. You think she was the same girl you saw in the woods with her mother?" said Max.

"Yeah, and Petey liked her, so I guess she wasn't there to scare me. She seemed awfully sad and acted like she wanted me to help her, somehow. She motioned with her hand for me to follow her. Maybe it had something to do with why she wanted to turn back in the woods?"

"Jinx, if you're sure they came from that early colonial period, maybe they're from the Lost Colony that your mom talked about."

"Wouldn't that be something? You're a genius!. It is beginning to connect now. It looks like we're the chosen ones to help our little girl ghost."

"Hey, wait a minute. What's this 'we' stuff? I don't want to meet any ghost." But Max laughed, and his blue eyes sparkled with excitement.

"Yeah, 'we.' My meeting you on the ferry was fate, kismet, meant to be. I can see us hanging out our wooden sign at our home office now. The *JMP History Mystery Detective Agency.* That has a nice ring to it."

"JMP?"

"Yeah. For Jinx, Max, and Petey. J-M-P, get it?"

"Hmmm, not bad. But I think it should be the *MPJ History Mystery Detective Agency.*"

Petey yipped his opinion. *"Woof, woof. PMJ–Petey, Max, Jinx, woof, woof!"*

"Oh great. Just what I need...you rotten guys ganging up on me, already."

With that, Max dragged me, pulling and kicking, the whole way down to the cold water. Of course, Petey helped so much by jumping around and barking his furry head off. But as I went under, I hooked Max's ankle and dragged him under, too. I'm no helpless girl detective, after all.

Chapter Nine:

The Campfire

Max and I built a roaring campfire together, that evening. We went back to the edge of the woods that bordered the beach and gathered some dry sticks and driftwood to start the fire.

"First, you lay a nest of twigs and dry grasses," Max said. I thought again about how patient he was when he taught me how to do something. "Next, you stand three larger logs on end and lean them into each other at the top, just like the framework for a teepee. Then you can place thinner pieces around the logs to form the sides. Here, you light it off, partner." He handed me a box of large matches.

After I ignited the twigs, the cone shape sucked the flames right up to the top, and within a minute the whole pile was aflame. We gave each other a high-five, very pleased with ourselves.

We let the fire calm down. The orange, yellow, and blue flames hissed and popped as long as we stirred the embers and added a few pieces of driftwood to feed it, now and then.

Mom walked over the dune, toting a picnic hamper. "Hi, gang. I brought the food. Hope you're hungry, because Max's mom sent lots of dogs."

Petey jumped up and searched all around. *"Dogs? Max has dogs?"*

"What's Petey barking about?" Mom said.

Max and I laughed. "He thinks you're talking about real dogs, Mom," I said.

Mom shook her head. "Oh, Petey, you're such a literal kind of dog, aren't you? I meant hotdogs."

Petey cocked his head at Mom. *"Ah-roooooo, no more hotdogs,"* he said. What a little clown.

Max helped Mom spread out the blanket and set the food on a tray. We grabbed long sticks, roasted the dogs, and wolfed down lots of them, slathered with yellow mustard. Petey was a good boy and stuck with his dog food and treats tonight.

After we ate, we were content to stare into the crackling flames in silence for a while. I reflected on the shell collecting, swimming, and fun we had during our first day at the beach. Our mom's had taken us back over to the ocean beach. Petey dug deep holes in the white sand, chased gulls away from our lunchtime picnic, and even went swimming with us.

I looked at my black and blue marks from attempting to surf for the first time ever. Max, impressed with my glider story, told me about his experience hang-gliding. He also spent the better part of the afternoon trying to teach Petey and me how to surf.

Max saw me checking out my battle scars.

"*Oooh,* those are some ugly bruises you got there," he said. "I'm sorry about that, but the good news is you really got the hang of it near the end."

"Yeah, right, Max. My surfing skills consisted of scrambling from my belly up to my knees. When I attempted to stand up in a balanced crouch, with my arms out like the graceful wings of a butterfly, I fell ker-plop, head over heels into those huge waves. That's how good I was."

"Don't get discouraged," Max said. "By the end of the summer, I'll have you turned into a real surfin' dude-ette."

"I love surfin,' I love surfin.' It's easy," said Petey. He crawled through the sand and rolled over on his back.

"Drat that fur-face Petey for getting the hang of it so fast," I said. "I still can't hang ten and ride the tide, but he sure can hang eighteen toes and brave the wave. And look at that self-satisfied smile on his little snoot, too."

Petey had us laughing as he rolled around kicking his legs in the air.

A sudden, chill breeze blew out from the woods behind us and stirred the flames. Mom, Max, and I all reached for our sweatshirts at the same time. The stars were a million sparkling diamonds in the night sky, and the gentle, lapping water rolled in from the sound like a lullaby. Petey came over and snuggled into my lap. I hugged him with both arms.

"What about that mysterious story now, you beach bums?" Mom said. "Somehow the time feels just right to tell you about the Lost Colony."

"Yeah, Mom. I'm curious about those people. They must have been really courageous to come way over here from England to start a new life. I guess this whole area was pretty wild back then, huh?"

"Wilder than wild, Jinx." Mom glanced away. "Max, what do you picture it looked like around here about four hundred years ago?" Mom said.

Max wrinkled his freckled nose, and his blue eyes took on a distant look. He scanned the sound and dunes, and then shifted his eyes to the wooded area. I could tell that he pictured a much different world. He scratched his sandy-colored head and began speaking in a low voice.

"I think the island was a pure, natural setting. I picture the sound and the ocean were clean and empty of any signs of people except for the Indians. No little cottages, no villages and stores, and definitely no beach bums and surfers." Max smiled at me when he mentioned surfers.

"I think the Indians came with silence and respect when they roamed the island. And I'm sure they didn't slather on sun tan lotion and lounge on the beach. They hunted animals in the woods and fished for survival, not for fun."

That really made me think. *The colonists from England had to build and make everything from scratch? The only supplies, tools, and clothes they had were what they could store on board that cramped ship that I had experienced in my vision. I'm not sure I would have been able to decide what to take along and what to leave behind.*

"So Mom, those people from England landed on an empty island with nothing here but beaches and woodland. They started life over again, didn't they? I guess the Indians weren't exactly thrilled with the colonists claiming their land."

Mom nodded. "I'm glad you two listened in history class. You're exactly right; they started their lives over again in hopes of owning land and building a better life than they had back in England. Some of the Natives were friendly, others mistrustful."

"And I know why they were mistrustful," Max said. "The Spanish and the English explorers didn't treat the Indians well at all." Max stared into the flickering flames as if mesmerized.

Mom looked at Max, then she glanced at me. I nodded, thinking of what Max had shared about Sir Richard Grenville and his soldiers burning down the Indian village over that missing silver cup.

Mom hesitated before she said, "Ready for the mystery of the Lost Colony? Ok, history fans, join me as we take a walk back in time. It was a dark and stormy night..."

"Oh, man. Here we go, Max, off on one of my mom's wild story telling flights."

"Shhhhhh. Hush up, Jinx. We want to hear this." Max and Petey both looked at me.

"Listen you guys. You're ganging up on me again..."

"SHHHHHHH!!!"

Mom began in a soft, low voice.

1587, The Story of The Lost Colony–Part 1

It was July 23, 1587. Off the coast of Roanoke Island, in America, John White felt shocked and dismayed. He had just heard an unbelievable command shouted down from

Captain Ferdinando, of the good ship Lyon, anchored in deep water.

Along with forty men, John had just been put aboard a smaller boat. Some of the men in the party were sailors; others were his colonists. They were to locate and pick up the fifteen men that had been left behind the previous year by Ralph Lane's party of English explorers to secure Fort Raleigh.

"Do not bring any of these planters back again. Leave them on the island. Summer is soon gone, and if we are to make it safely back to Europe before winter's harsh storms are upon us, we must make haste to leave within a few days. We will not be taking them inland. The rest of John White's party will disembark on Roanoke Island in the morn," roared the captain.

Not being taken inland? But he was to be governor of these brave colonists when they reached Virginia. The City of Raleigh, named in honor of their benefactor, Sir Walter Raleigh, would be founded.

These courageous men and women had given up their safe lives in England, left most of their worldly possessions behind, and traveled across treacherous seas for six weeks to the New World. Here, they expected to be given 500 acres for homesteading and a greater voice in the government. This was a king's treasure in the minds of the humble colonists.

John White put his hands on his hips, and then threw a fist at the captain. He cared not that his anger boiled over. "What do you mean by this change of plans, Captain Ferdinando? You were paid a tidy sum from Sir Walter Raleigh to deliver us the whole way up into the Chesapeake Bay to the Virginia colony. It won't take us but a day to check on the soldiers left behind here last year to hold down the fort. This is the final insult. You have not listened to anything I have asked of you this whole trip."

"Bah, John White. Who was it that delayed the start of the trip by two weeks? You are the one who had us stop at two ports before we even left Europe. What were you thinking, man? You know 'tis important to watch the time of year and the prevailing winds to insure a good voyage," said Ferdinando. He shrugged his shoulders and spit a glob of phlegm onto the deck.

White grabbed his cloth hat from his head and twisted it in his fists. He'd like to wring Ferdinando's neck, instead. "I wonder, good captain, if you had planned this whole time to prey upon the Spanish galleons loaded with treasure for the King of Spain, instead of delivering us to Virginia. It seems you have tried to doom our English colony from the start," White said. "You're nothing but a pirate." But he knew he was beaten. "Enough of this idle chatter, men. We have a job to do, so let us row in to the island." He turned his back on Ferdinando and pulled his hat back onto his head.

"You wound me with your harsh words, John White. I'm not a pirate, I'm a privateer for our good Queen Elizabeth." Ferdinando held his hands over his heart, as if in great pain, and then he laughed.

White spoke in a low voice to his son-in-law, Ananias. "Now what am I to do? What should I tell our colonists who trust me as their leader? Our plans have been drastically changed by that command, for I really have no authority over Captain Simon Ferdinando. By the laws of sailing ships, the captain rules above everyone else."

Ananias glared at the sailors who rowed the boat. They stared back with bold grins, having enjoyed all of the fighting between their captain and White.

Ananias turned away from the sailors and spoke even softer than White. "There is nothing to be done, sir. We must make the best of it and move into the fort to prepare for the coming winter. We will hope Manteo and his village will help us with food."

They eyed the approaching terrain: a curving, sandy beach, with wild vegetation leading back to thick woodland. There was no welcoming smoke from the fort area, and no soldiers coming out, excited to see them.

John White had a bad feeling about being abandoned on this wild island so late in July, with few supplies to sustain them throughout a long fall and winter. He looked at his son-in-law. He was a tiler and bricklayer of the yeoman, or middling, class in England. His work had brought in enough money for a comfortable life, and to purchase ship's passage for he and his wife, Eleanor, to accompany their father and father-in-law on this journey, but Ananias certainly had never hunted or fished to feed his family—and judging by the furrows on his brow, well he knew his skills were lacking in those areas.

"Aye, son, we will make the best of it," White said. He took a huge breath of air and blew it out.

The boat hit the shallow waters and scraped against pebbles and sand. The sailors jumped out to pull it further up onto the beach. Their job being finished for now, they moved close together to discuss the situation.

"To be sure Capt'n wants to look for a few Spanish ships to scuttle for their treasure, what do ya think?" said a sailor, to his mates. He wore a headband and had tattoos of mermaids and sea serpents that wrapped around his arms.

"More riches for us than this trip promised, if we do," agreed another. The whole lot of sailors was a ragged, scary-looking bunch.

"This way, men," White ordered. Whatever am I doing in this position, he thought. I'm not a leader; I'm an artist.

White had done spectacular paintings during the English exploration trips he had accompanied the prior two years. He captured the wildlife and the highly organized Indian village life here in America as no man had before him. That had won him Sir Walter Raleigh's favor to be appointed governor of the colony.

He led the troops toward a grown-over path that entered into the wooded area. It was a beautiful, hot summer day. The small waves in the sound rolled in to the beach, while gulls called out, seeming to laugh at them. Haaaaaa–ha, ha, ha, haaaaaaaa.

The men hesitated at the edge of the woods before they pushed into the dim interior. Their faces soon glistened with sweat in the humidity. Mosquitoes and tiny gnats swarmed and bit with a vengeance. No one felt like talking, so the insect and bird chirping sounded magnified and annoying.

White held up his arm to halt them. They looked left and right, over their shoulders–nothing. They moved on, hacking and chopping through the tangled vines. White held up his arm, again. This time, they all experienced the eerie feeling of being watched, but they saw no one.

"Let's push on," White ordered. "Fort Raleigh is bound to be nearby."

After an eternal five more minutes of swatting bugs, wiping sweat from brows, and tripping over vegetation, the group straggled into a clearing, with the high, wooden post walls of the fort before them.

Fort Raleigh was deserted. The forest had taken over; it had grown everywhere. Tentacles of vines wrapped themselves in between every niche of the fort. The few rough houses had partially collapsed. Some of the fence had fallen over. None of the soldiers left behind appeared to great them. White's men twisted and turned, expecting any minute to be attacked by the Natives.

"Spread out, men. Go with a partner and search the area around the fort. Look for any clues that might tell us what happened to the Queen's soldiers," White said.

It wasn't more than half an hour later that a shout was heard. "Over here, Governor White," called a colonist.

He was found staring at a tree that had been split by lightning and fallen over. The anxious men ran to the spot and stopped in their tracks. There, by the downed tree, laid a skeleton, still half clothed in metal armor, it's skull grinning at them in death. Nearby were a few arrowheads.

A few men did the best they could to bury the dead soldier, while the rest of the party continued to search. Come sundown, they met on the beach, discouraged and scared. No other sign of the fourteen missing soldiers had been found.

John White left most of his men on the beach, as ordered, and returned to the Lyon. The men who were not permitted to return aboard the ship prepared their campfires on the beach for the night, fearful and apprehensive. They kept watch with their weapons ready the whole night. No one slept.

The next day, the clouds scudded quickly across the sky, and distant thunder rumbled. Governor White gathered his colonists to make the announcement.

"We will be staying on Roanoke Island for the winter," White said. "Lord willing, we must repair and build shelters as needed. Then in the spring we will make our way inland to Virginia.

"So, make haste, my brave colonists. There is much to do. You wanted adventure, and so you shall have it. Now step lively and with good spirit," John encouraged them.

By August the colonists settled into their temporary City of Raleigh on Roanoke Island. They had only one true Indian friend, Manteo, of the Croatoan tribe.

Manteo and Wanchese, one of the weroances, or chiefs, from the Roanoac tribe, had journeyed back to England with the explorers a few years back to be introduced to the Queen. But only Manteo remained loyal to the colonists Wanchese had chosen not to trust them.

To show their gratitude for Manteo's loyalty, the colonists baptized him into the Church of England on August 13th. They christened him Lord of Roanoke and Dasemunkepeuc, his home village.

The colonists tried to keep their spirits high, but the tasks of building shelters and hunting for food for a whole colony of people seemed to be insurmountable. By daylight hope was fragile. At night, every noise that came from the wilderness surrounding them caused great fear. They needed more than Manteo's promise of help. They needed supplies from England as quickly as possible. And they needed to survive a harsh winter in this new land before those badly needed supplies could arrive.

The logs in the campfire shifted and sent a shower of bright sparks up into the night air. Max and I practically jumped out of our skins at this unexpected noise. It had been so quiet on the beach while Mom's tale mesmerized us.

I looked around, shivering with apprehension. I tried to imagine what it must have felt like to be abandoned on an island with few provisions, so far from home.

"It doesn't look good for the colonists, Mom," I said.

"That's for sure," added Max. "What happened? Did Governor White get back to Roanoke Island? Did they get the supplies they needed? Did the Indians attack?"

"Yeah, Mom, did John White ever get to see his granddaughter, Virginia, again? How did the whole colony disappear?"

"Whoa, you two. Give me a chance to catch my breath," said Mom.

I gave a big yawn and stretched my arms high. That caused Max and Petey to yawn, too. Mom laughed as she caught the yawns going around the campfire.

A wind came up and we noticed clouds had appeared that scudded over the moon. A flash of lightning far off caused a faint rumble in the distance. A thunderstorm was headed our way.

"We have plenty of time to tell mysteries. How about if we meet here tomorrow night after supper, and I'll tell you the rest of the story?" Mom suggested.

We all yawned again and agreed that the first day had finally worn us out. Max and I lagged behind Mom as we headed back to the cottages.

Max's brow furrowed. "I hope I'm exhausted enough to sleep without any weird vision adventures like I had last night," Max said.

"I know what you mean," I said. "This strange stuff happening to us is really scary, but since I met you it's somehow easier. I don't feel so alone," I said. I didn't look at Max. I hoped he didn't think I was getting all gushy and girly on him.

Ohmigosh! That's exactly what he must have thought, because his ears turned bright red and he gave me a little shove.

"All right, MacKenzie, I agree. We'll figure this all out...*um...t-t-together.*" He stammered like he'd never talked to a girl before.

The lightning flashed a bit closer. Petey yipped and flipped and barked. *"Come on, you guys, let's race. Beat ya back, beat ya back."*

So, Max and I took off and chased Petey back over the dune. I hoped we'd all get a good night's sleep. *Please, no little ghost girl for me tonight,* I thought.

Chapter Ten:

Surfin' Disaster

Max was glad he had a good couple of night's sleep, and the terror of the wild dream was starting to fade. It was another brilliant summer day on the Outer Banks. A thunderstorm over night had freshened the earth and brought some great waves on the ocean beach. Max's dad drove Jinx and him back over the sound to Nags Head for some more surfing lessons and swimming.

Max leaned his head back against the car seat and sighed. The windows were all rolled down to allow for the refreshing breezes to cool them off.

"Man, I love the way it smells after a thunderstorm—kinda fresh and stuff," he said.

Jinx sniffed the air from her seat beside him in his family's car. "Yeah, that was quite a storm last night. But thank goodness it's nice today." She leaned forward, "Thanks again for taking Max and me to the ocean beach, Mr. Myers. Max says the waves are going to be awesome for surfing lessons."

"You're welcome, Jinx," Max's dad said. "Did the storm keep you awake last night?"

"Not really. I woke up a couple of times when the thunder was really loud, but I went right back to sleep. Of course, Petey slept right through it." Jinx had a firm grip on Petey's collar as he hung his head out the window. His ears flew in the wind.

Petey pulled his head and gave her a big lick on the nose. *"What storm, what storm?"*

Max grinned. "Not me. I'm happy to report that I slept right through it. No dreams, no thunder, nothing. That was nice—for a change, he added under his breath.

They pulled to a stop at the local surf shop so Jinx could look at the beginner surfboards. Petey and Max's dad waited on a bench outside.

Max could tell by his reaction that Jack, the owner of the store, was glad to see Max again. "Hey, Max. When did you get in? It's great to see you again, this year," Jack said.

He was a friendly, giant of a man. His dark hair hung to his shoulders, and his sunburned nose peeled.

"Hey, Jack, nice to see you, too. We got here a couple days ago, but we did some sightseeing, first. How's the surf, today?" Max said.

"Surf's up, according to the boys. Expect some giants by late afternoon. You were gettin' good, by the end of last summer. Gonna try to shoot the tube this year?"

Max felt his cheeks redden. Great. Of course Jack asked him that with Jinx right beside him, eager to hear what his answer would be! He gulped, then gave Jack a weak smile. "Um... I guess this is the year to make it happen." He tipped his head toward Jinx, "Oh, yeah, and this is my friend, Jinx. I'm giving her some surfing tips."

Jinx smiled. "Hi, Jack. What's the tube?" she asked both Max and Jack.

Jack leaned forward on the counter between them. "It's the most exciting surf ride of all, Jinx. The tube is the space inside a huge, breaking wave, between the lip and the face. Sometimes you can't even see the surfer if he's in the tube.

"Think of the space inside of a barrel. The top of the barrel is the top of the wave curling over," Jack added. His eyes gleamed with excitement, thinking about it. "So, you goin' for it, Max?"

"Sounds dangerous," Jinx said, looking at her friend, Max and lost her smile.

Max didn't meet her eyes. Once again he felt embarrassed to be challenged by Jack in front of Jinx.

Max pretended he hadn't heard Jack's last question. "Hey, I need some board wax, and Jinx and I are gonna check out the beginner surf boards," Max said, as he turned and walked down the first aisle. Jinx followed him.

"Max, don't try that tube thing just so I can see it. I already think you're an awesome surfer." Max could tell that she knew he was embarrassed.

Max shook his head and grinned. "I don't know–I'd be tempted to try it if I saw some great waves. It's the challenge and excitement of it..."

After they cruised the aisles and looked at the boards, Max paid for the wax, and they turned toward the door.

"Later, Dude," Jack called after them. They grinned and waved good-bye.

The teens joined Max's Dad and Petey on the sidewalk. Petey jumped all over them and greeted them like they'd been gone for days. *"Hi ya, hi ya! Are we goin' to the beach now? Are we goin' to the beach?"* Petey said. They stooped to pet him.

"Hey, Dad. Ready to catch some waves?" Max asked. They walked a few blocks out to the dunes and beach.

"I'll go down the beach a bit to surf," Dad said. "Don't get out of my sight, please." It was obvious that he didn't want Max and Jinx to think he was hovering over them too closely.

Max rolled his eyes. "Dad, I'll make sure we're safe." *First Jack challenges me, now Dad embarrasses me. I can't win, today.*

"I know you're reliable, Max. But I'm responsible for you both. So humor me, please, and stay in sight."

"Okay, Dad." Max was in his element. He loved any sport with a board: surfing, skim-boarding, skateboarding, snowboarding; Max was a natural.

Petey ran circles around their feet. *"Hey Dude, hey Dude, can I surf today, can I?"*

They laughed at the excited terrier. "Not today, Petey, we need you to guard the beach," Jinx said. She patted his head. They laid their towels on the sand.

Petey barked at the curious gulls, taking his guard duty to heart. *"Go away, gulls. Nothing here for you, bark, bark, bark."* He sat down on the towels to watch.

Yesterday, Max had taught Jinx how to lie on her board so her balance was perfect. She had used Max's beginner board in the sound to practice. They had marked the spot where her chin would lay with a red marker.

"Okay, Jinx, review time," Max said. "What's the problem if the tip of your board rises above the water when you're lying on the board?"

"Too much body weight to the back makes the board cork, or the tip rise out of the water," Jinx said.

"Right. What's the problem if the board's nose digs into the water?"

"Your body weight is shifted too far front. It's called pearling. Either way is trouble if a wave hits you. Your board should lie level in the water," Jinx said. She was proud of herself.

"Good! Today we practice paddling. Don't worry about trying to stand up. That'd be like a baby trying to run before he can walk without falling over," Max said.

He saw Jinx wince at the analogy of the baby. "Okay...bad analogy. Let's say surfing is like any other sport–there are basic skills to learn and practice that will lead into being able to stand up and catch a wave.

Max kicked at the sand in front of him, then quietly said, "I pushed you way too fast the other day. I don't know what I was thinking. My Dad really gave it to me for trying to get you up on the board too soon. It can be dangerous if you go out there and try to surf without understanding the basics. Sorry about that, Okay?"

Jinx smiled and gave him a "thumbs up." "Okay, Coach, what's next?"

"Let's go out past the breakers, and I'll show you how to paddle."

Max and Jinx ran through the crashing waves, carrying their boards to the side with both hands. Jinx wore a Velcro wrist strap and tie that connected to her board for safety. When they were past the breakers, they both pushed up onto their boards. Jinx checked where her chin mark was so her board would be balanced in the water.

"Lookin' good, Jinx. Let's practice paddling parallel to the beach, out here in the swells. You want to use your arms like you're swimming the crawl stroke; first one arm, then the other, back and forth. That way you keep up a steady pace. It makes it easier to catch a wave. Always keep your head up. Watch."

Max paddled his board his board a few yards away, then turned and paddled back. Jinx nodded.

"I'll try," she said. She started off using alternate arms and was surprised how smooth the ride was.

"Keep your head high," Max reminded her.

Jinx paddled back and grabbed her board, grinning at Max. "This is fun! Thanks for being so patient and for...well...not teasing me."

"Let's paddle for awhile to practice...oh, wait. Look at my dad!" Max said.

They turned in time to see Max's dad catch a perfect, large wave and ride it all the way in to the beach, where he jumped off his board. They cheered and clapped when he turned around and waved to them. Petey ran up and down the beach, barking and doing flips.

Max hoped that Jinx didn't notice how jittery he felt, all of a sudden. Here it came again, that wired feeling of his body being electrified. *Something strange is going to happen, I can feel it coming on. Maybe I should call it quits on surfing for today,* he thought. But they paddled down the beach for a bit, then paddled back up toward their towels and equipment on the beach.

"Phew," Jinx said, "My arm muscles are really burning. I can see that surfing is a great workout. I'm going in."

Suddenly Jinx shuddered and the light got fuzzy. *What's happening,* she thought. *It's Max, something's wrong.* She looked at her friend–he had a darkness surrounding him. Jinx shook off the strange feeling and looked back at Max. This time he looked normal.

"You coming in with me?" she said. "Maybe we should both head back to the beach and rest."

Max nodded. "Okay, but I want to catch a wave and surf in. Meet you back on the beach." He waved. Max sat on his board, trying to shake his nervous feeling. *It's like I have to squeeze all my muscles and then relax them. I don't like this wired feeling at all,* he thought. *Concentrate on the waves, that's what I'll do.*

The swells and waves hadn't lessened in height during the afternoon. If anything, they appeared to be getting larger, just like Jack had told them. Max's Dad yelled and waved his arms at Max to come in. Max nodded.

Max looked over his shoulder at a building wall of water. *This looks like a good one. Wow, it could be that giant wave I'm looking for; maybe I can catch my first run through the tube.* His heart pounded in his rib cage. He began paddling, faster and faster, then jumped up to his feet.

Exhilarated, Max caught the wave and surfed down the front. He glanced to his right and saw the wave begin to curl over. His eyes widened. *Amazing! I can see the tunnel–I'm goin' for it!* He crouched low and shot into the tunnel as the giant wall curved high, over his back.

I'm inside the tube; I've done it! Uh oh...I misjudged this wave...it's crashing too soon. I'm loosin' it...

Max tumbled off of his surfboard, inside of the giant tube. Oh brother, I'm a gonner. It's going to slam me, he thought. But instead of feeling the wet, cold ocean water, he felt like he was being swirled and spun through a dark tunnel to...where? Where was he headed this time?

Chapter Eleven:

Nightmare Attack

Who's trying to pull me back through the tube? Hey! Leave me alone! Max's thoughts whirled and jumbled. He vaguely heard soft voices from far, far away and felt fingers probing the back of his head. *Ouch...! Hurts. Why are you pounding on my chest. Ow! Stop. Please stop!* Max coughed, and choked up brackish water. He tried to open his eyes, but it was just so, *so* hard. *Leave me alone,* he thought. *Why won't you just leave me alo...* He felt the darkness take him again—he swirled away into the past, and became an observer once more through the eyes of someone else...

Roanoke Island– Fall 1585 to Spring 1586

Wanchese, one of Wingina's chiefs, watched the white men working on the fort. He was well hidden behind the brush. He knew some of the men by name, and he was quickly learning to know them by character. Some, like Ralph Lane, were not to be trusted. Wanchese had learned to speak some English the year he visited England. So, what he heard Lane discussing with his chief men caused him dismay.

Ralph Lane was in complete charge of the 107 men left behind on the island of Roanoke. The new fort had been built along with several houses for the men to live in. They were to establish England's hold on land in America until a more permanent colony could be established up in the Chesapeake Bay area the following year.

Along his military chain of command was Master Edward Stafford, head of the first company. Captain John Vaughn headed the second company of men. Master Thomas Harvie, a London grocer, was in charge of the supplies. He dispensed the food to be eaten and supervised trading with the Indians. Then there was Thomas Heriot, who was the scientist, historian, and interpreter with the Indians. He had taught Manteo and Wanchese English, and learned their language while doing lessons. John White was along again as artist.

Wanchese listened to Ralph Lane speak. "Men, the chief weroance of the

Roanoac coastal Indians, Wingina, is plotting a large attack against us. I hear he is rallying hundreds of Indians from other tribes to head to Roanoke Island and our fort. His father is an old, infirm man–we don't have to worry about old Ensenore. But Wingina's brother, Granganimeo, and that ingrate, Wanchese, are forces to be worried over. They all need to be eliminated, even the old man. And to think that we took Wanchese to England...it's a wonder he didn't kill the Queen."

Captain John Vaughn scowled. "But Lane, upon what do you base your information of a plot against us? Wingina has offered much of his own tribe's food supplies for the winter to us. He has cooperated in every way, teaching the men hunting and fishing skills. I should think we'd want to keep the peace with the natives, not stir up fights."

Now, Lane scowled at his Captain. "How dare you question your superior, Vaughn? I have my ways of knowing what goes on in the Indian villages and their secret councils. I say they are a dangerous lot that must be taken out. We go in the morn. Have the men ready by the boats."

Wanchese turned on silent tread and made his way to his canoe. He must warn his village.

Wingina and his advisors sat in his lodge, around the campfire. The discussed in low voices what to do with the troubling news Wanchese brought to them.

"We must hit them by surprise before they arrive at the village," said one of the advisors.

Wingina shook his head, "I think that plan is unwise," he said. They have powerful guns that kill quickly–our arrows will never stand up to the powerful weapons they carry. We must talk and convince Lane that we have no plan to attack. I do not like them here, any more than you. But peaceful ways may be the best approach."

Old father Ensenore nodded his head and puffed on his pipe. His eyes were the wet, faded eyes of a very old man. A young boy slipped into the lodge and whispered into Ensenore's ear.

Ensenore lifted his arm and the lodge fell silent. "The boy says the white leader and his men are marching into the far end of the village. Let them come and talk with us." He went back to puffing his pipe.

Wingina spoke to another young man at his side. "Tell Lane to come to our fire to talk." The young brave walked over to the entrance, his face solemn and unreadable, and he ducked through the entrance to do his duty.

Wanchese shook his head. He jumped to his feet and grabbed his bow and sack of arrows. "Wingina, these men have no honor–they are not here to talk–they are here to kill. You must give the alert for battle," he warned.

But Wingina crossed his arms. "No, Wanchese, we will listen to what Ralph Lane has to say." Wanchese scowled and slipped out the back door of the lodge.

Soon they could hear the tramping and marching of the troops, dressed in their metal armor and helmets, swords and guns by their sides. They marched close to Wingina's lodge and halted at the command.

Lane, along with some of his commanders, entered the lodge and saw Wingina, his old father, his brother Granganimeo, and several other important weroances sitting together. What a perfect opportunity to strike, Lane thought. All in one blow, and the chief leaders of the Indians are gone.

Before the Indians could great them, Lane shouted the prearranged signal for attack: "Christ our victory!"

The soldiers burst in like charging bulls; gunshots roared, and knives flashed. In the whole village, pandemonium broke out. Wingina fell to the ground right away. Old Ensenore lay dead in a puddle of blood, and Granganimeo was stabbed and shot dead.

Wanchese fought along with the other Indians, but their arrows were no match for the power of Lane's troops with guns.

In the chaos, Wingina suddenly jumped to his feet and ran into the woods. He had pretended to be dead, hoping to make a run for safety. Ralph Lane's personal servant, the Irishman, Nugent, became the hero of the day. He ran into the woods after the Indian chief and finally returned with Wingina's head, which he proudly presented to Ralph Lane.

Late that day, after the soldiers marched away with their chief's head and most of their stores of corn and beans, Wanchese helped the remaining villagers prepare the slain bodies for proper burial ceremonies. Fire and hatred smoldered in his breast.

Weeks after the massacre, Wanchese crept near to the fort on Roanoke Island again and waited by the old oak with a hole on one side. Manteo had sent Wanchese a message to meet him there on the next full moon.

Wanchese thought of the past. He and Manteo had met when they were boys, left alone here on the island to fish and hunt and survive, to prove to their village elders they were worthy of becoming men. They had met by accident when a third tribe of enemy hunters chased Manteo to kill him. Wanchese, instead of hiding and staying safe, joined Manteo to fire arrow after arrow through the air toward the chests of the enemy. The enemy braves retreated and left the island. That was well received at home in their villages for both of the young men–Wanchese of the Roanoacs, and Manteo of the Croatoans. They swore to become blood brothers, forever.

Then came the time when the white explorers landed on their soil and laid claim to the Indian's land. Manteo and he had even traveled together to England to meet their Queen and learn about the ways of the white people. Manteo was fascinated with the white men and their ways. But Wanchese knew the lives of his people would be forever changed for the worse if they allowed the white men to continue to come to America.

Now, years later, the white men from far away had brought trouble to their homeland. It was obvious to Wanchese that the white men intended to stay, living on the land belonging to their tribes. On one hand, the white men pretended to need help to survive, on the other, they stole supplies and killed the villagers. Why could his brother, Manteo, not see this duplicity?

Wanchese felt sad. I must do the hard thing tonight, he thought. His heart would break, but it was time. He felt a presence and turned quickly, reaching for his knife. In the patch of moonlight stood a laughing man, his blood brother, Manteo.

"Manteo, you are still as stealthy as a fox, like when you were a boy first visiting this island. And I was too buried in my thoughts tonight, a dangerous thing. How are you, my brother?"

The men placed their hands on each other's shoulders and smiled.

Then Manteo's face changed to sadness. "I am well, Wanchese. How does it go in your village?" Manteo knew there had been a terrible raid by the white soldiers.

Wanchese dropped his hands and shook his head. "Not well. My people are frightened and furious with the actions of the white men. They mourn their family members who were killed in the attack. And now word has reached far and wide that Ralph Lane and his soldiers have attacked and killed Wingina, our royal weroance, chief of all the Roanoacs.

Manteo dropped his head. He knew these actions of his white friends caused ties between the Indians and the white men to be forever severed. "I have heard this terrible news. Ralph Lane is not a good man. But not all of them are like him. Remember our trip to see the Queen of England? We were treated like royalty," Manteo said.

Wanchese stood tall, feet apart and arms crossed over his chest. He was quick to anger. "You were taken with their ways, not I. I think you now must have some white blood in you, the way you defend them. You know that many more whites will come and settle here. They will use us and take our foods and our land. They will push us away; maybe even try to kill us all. No good will come of this. We must rally to kill these invaders, and send a message back to their country to stay away. Will your tribe join us, Manteo, before it is too late?"

Manteo shook his head, his eyes pleading for his blood brother to listen. "Wanchese, we can offer a truce to the whites. I think we can still work out a peace, one that can benefit us all. They have weapons and goods to trade for our help in feeding them. They can teach us, teach our children many new and good things, like reading their books for knowledge beyond our land. And they need to learn the ways of living in our land, hunting and planting crops that will thrive: corn, beans, and gourds. They want to live well off the land, like we do. White men with families, women and children will be coming soon. Can we not live together in peace?"

Manteo grabbed Wanchese by the shoulders again. "My Brother, will you join me in helping the white men when they come to settle?"

Wanchese shook his head, sadly. He pushed Manteo's hands away and stepped back. "I have tried, Manteo, to reason with you. We are far apart on this issue. I can no longer be your Brother. I am sorry."

The two men stared at each other for a long moment. Then Wanchese turned and slipped away into the shadows of the woods, disappearing from Manteo's life.

"Manteo, my brother, listen to me...we cannot trust the white men, please..."

Max struggled, still believing he was Wanchese. Something held his arms and legs down, so he kicked and floundered.

"Max, welcome back from wherever you were, son." His dad gently helped Max get untangled from the crisp, white sheets of a hospital bed. Max's mom and Jinx watched him from their chairs, both with worried eyes.

Max sat up and looked around in confusion. "But, where am I? What happened?" He realized his head was pounding and gingerly felt around his skull. Max winced when he touched a thick pad on the back of his head. Surfing–they had been surfing.

"That huge wave came out of nowhere. Oh, Dad, I was in the tube, but...but it took me somewhere far away, like, like back in the past. And I was an Indian named Wanchese." Max blinked his eyes, thinking. "Am I going crazy, Dad?"

His dad glanced at Jinx and Max's mother.

"It's okay, Dad. Jinx can hear this," Max said.

"Max, you're not going crazy. There's a reason you're experiencing all of these dreams."

"I told you, they're not dreams, Dad. It's something more than that. I'm seeing these things through the eyes of people from long ago, like I slid into their bodies." Max slapped the sheets in frustration.

" You're right, Max. We actually did lose you for a moment or two," Dad said.

"Do you mean I died or something?" Max asked. His face was solemn.

"No, I mean we really lost you," Dad said. "That wave was like a rogue wave, huge and terrifying. They don't see giant waves like that around here very often, they told me. After it crested, we looked for you. Your...your board washed in, but you were nowhere to be found. Gone.

"Then all of a sudden, there you were, lying way up on the beach, totally out of it. I had dialed 911, so the medics started CPR right away, and then they brought you to the hospital. The doctor said you were fine, except for your head wound. You might have a concussion. But you were still totally out. You looked like you weren't here with us."

"Yeah, because *I was way back there with the Indians and explorers*. John Lane wasn't a very nice guy, by the way. Jinx, we gotta talk," Max said. He sat up again and turned to her, wincing as his body groaned with aches and pains from being tossed and turned and smacked around by the giant wave.

Jinx blew out a big sigh. "I'm glad you're feeling better, Max. Your dad and I were frantic when we couldn't see you. It was very strange how you got by us. We found you way up on a dune, and it was dry up there–the waves certainly didn't carry you up there. You just...uh... appeared." She stopped and looked off into nowhere, puzzled by the events.

Max raised his eyebrows and tilted his head, looking back at his dad and mom to explain what happened.

"Max, you father has something to tell you. It's pretty bizarre and may upset you. But we are always here to help you through these new situations." Mom glanced at Max's dad for help.

"Max, you are a...uh...you're a...time traveler," his dad began. "It runs in our family." Max burst out laughing in relief, and Jinx joined in.

His father certainly didn't expect that reaction. He looked back and forth between the teens.

Then Max sobered up when he thought about the consequences. "That explains all of the strange stuff happening to me." He buried his face in his hands. "A time traveler. Why me? I think I'd rather be a plain old boy with no weird talents."

"I know. That's how I felt when Grandpa talked with me the first time. I wanted nothing to do with time traveling. I just wanted to stay home and read my comic books," Max's dad said.

Max raised his head, his mouth open. "You're a time traveler, too?"

Dad nodded. "I was. My powers faded as I grew older. If I really had to, I think I could still go back, but I'm not called to action like I was as a boy. You're very special, Max. It's your turn to help."

"That's what my mom told me this summer," said Jinx. She had been nodding in understanding.

Max's parents had forgotten Jinx was in the room; they were so intent upon Max and his reaction to the strange news.

"Oh, wow! Two of you to worry about?" Max's mother said. Both teens nodded, with big round eyes and serious faces.

"Okay, Dad. We can talk more later," said Max's mother. "And I guess we'd better have a talk with Jinx's mom, too. Let's go get some coffee and let Max rest. Jinx, want to join us for a milkshake?" she added.

Jinx shook her head. "Thanks, but I'll stay here with Max."

Max's mother smiled. "We'll be back in a bit. Max has no food restrictions, so we'll bring you both milkshakes. What flavor?"

"Strawberry," they both answered at once, then looked at each other and laughed.

When his parents were gone, Max turned tired eyes on his friend. "Jinx, that tube through the wave was some kind of tunnel to the past. It grabbed me, and I had no choice. I don't like having no control over what happens to me. What if I can't get back?"

Jinx chewed on a fingernail, and then said, "Well...maybe things are only out of control right now because...um... we're new at it. It should get better, right? More under control the more we do it. And, at least we have each other...It's kinda nice to know someone else is experiencing the same weird stuff." She laid her hand on Max's arm for a brief moment, and he smiled.

"Yeah, we'll figure it out," Max said. "We're smack in the middle of a very historical place. You can feel the strangeness in the mist. People keep appearing to us. I think everything I'm seeing and the things you're going through are very much tied together. I've got a lot to tell you about the soldiers who first came here from England, and their interactions with the Indians. I saw another English attack on an Indian village. "

"And it all has to do with England's first colony," Jinx added with certainty.

"I think we'll let the surfing lessons go for a week or so, just 'til my hard head heals up," Max said. He yawned as his eyes closed.

Jinx agreed. She curled up in the chair near his bed. *This is one strange summer,* she thought. *I hope we survive it.* Her eyes felt heavy with fatigue, and her arm muscles and leg muscles felt very strained from the new exercise on the surfboard. Before long, she nodded off and joined Max in a restful sleep, while an eerie mist swirled in from the ocean and surrounded the building.

Chapter Twelve:

A Visit from Orville

A few days after Max's latest trip into history, we floated around in an inflatable boat in the backwaters of the sound, since he still wasn't supposed to get his stitches wet. It was quiet and gave us a chance to discuss what had been going on. Nothing weird had bothered either one of us since Max's surfing disaster.

I rowed our boat some and let it drift into the reeds and cattails. We talked about what we both had seen, so far.

"Well, I found myself in the bottom of a sailing ship heading to America with the settlers from England, met Orville Wright and the fly boys, saw a lady from long ago with her little girl running through the woods, like Little Red Riding Hood, and had the same little girl visit Petey and me," I muttered.

"Right," Max said. "And I was John White, artist for the Queen, who marched along with Sir Richard Grenville's soldiers to burn out a whole Indian village over a stupid, missing silver cup.

"Then I got to take the best surf ride of my life through the tube, only the tube took me back to the 1500s again. That time, I witnessed another horrible raid on an Indian village that killed Wingina, the weroance of all the Roanoac Indian tribes, along with his family. And I saw it through the eyes of Wanchese. These visions are adding a whole new meaning to the term "walk a few miles in their shoes." I'm definitely seeing things from the Native American point of view."

We thought about that as we drifted, dragging our fingers through the soothing water.

"What's the word *weroance* mean, Max?" I asked. "Is it like the head or chief of a group?"

Max nodded. He felt the back of his head, where his stitches were located. He had told me they still pulled and felt uncomfortable.

"That second raid was conducted by Ralph Lane, over some imagined plot that the Indians were gathering to kill the soldiers at the fort," Max said. "I believe Ralph Lane made it all up to have an excuse to raid the Indian village. I guess they figured if they take out all of the big chiefs, the Indians would be scattered and less dangerous without their leaders."

"At least now we know all of these people in our visions were part of England's attempt to get a foothold in the new land of America," I said. "The things you saw were before they sent the women and children. You were right when you said Ralph Lane wasn't a very nice guy. He was part of that mentality that wanted to show the Indians who would be boss."

"You know, when I was seeing things through Wanchese's eyes, I really felt his sadness when he broke off ties with his blood brother, Manteo. They parted ways because Wanchese didn't trust the white men, and Manteo wanted to continue to help them, even after they killed so many Native Americans. Why do you think Manteo stayed with the colonists?" Max said.

I turned sideways so I could put my legs over the side of the boat and dip my feet in the cool water while I thought. The sun caused the rippling water to look like sparkling gems.

"I don't know. It doesn't make sense, does it? Maybe he liked the importance of being their interpreter. Or maybe he hoped the white settlers would bring good things for his people," I said. I pulled my wet feet back into the boat and turned to face Max.

"We're getting lots of background about the Lost Colony, but we're not getting answers to the mystery of what the little girl wants from us. Much less what happened to the colony. Mom says let's have that campfire tonight, and she'll tell us more of the story."

We floated on, listening to the calls of the wildlife. Max read from our field guide about the birds of the southeast Atlantic coast. We whispered because everything was so quiet and calm. Petey lay curled up in Max's lap. He lifted his head now and then and sniffed the air.

"Look, over there," Max said. He pointed at a huge, wading bird. I sat up as quietly as I could, hoping I wouldn't scare away the bird. I had never seen such a large bird. It stood very tall and was covered in white feathers, except for its wrinkled, bald, head. The bird's long legs were jointed to bend backward. It picked its pink feet up and down and scared the little fish forward for its beak to gobble up.

Max scanned the guide with his finger, looking for its name. He gasped, "A Wood Stork–they're endangered. We are so lucky to see it!"

We all felt the difference in the air at the same time. Our surroundings wavered in and out of focus, once, twice. Petey sat up, alert now, his paws up over the side of the boat. A gentle mist rolled around us, touching our cheeks with tiny pearls of moisture.

The Wood Stork opened its giant wings, then folded them close to its body. It turned its head and stared at us. "There are things you still must see to understand the past," it said in a squawky voice. Then its form wavered and disappeared in the mist. Petey waved a paw but didn't bark.

Now, I pointed. Over on the bank, in the swirly mist, stood a tall man in a Hawaiian shirt waving at us. His ears stuck straight out from his head, and we could see his large, curled moustache. "It's Orville, Max," I whispered. "He's come to visit me, just like he promised."

Max's mouth dropped open. "But that guy's wearing a Hawaiian shirt," he said. "Why would he wear a Hawaiian shirt?"

I laughed. "So he won't scare us, I suppose. Maybe he likes the bright colors, who knows," I said. I realized I was nervously giggling. *I know he wants us to go with him, back in time. I really don't want to do this,* I thought.

"It's okay, Jinx. We'll both go along with him. We'll do it together," Max said.

I forgot that Max could read my thoughts. I felt braver, safer with him by my side. Petey wiggled all over. *"Woof, woof. Hi, Orville."* He gave little yips of pleasure.

I rowed in toward the bank, and Max threw the rope to Orville, who caught it and pulled us up onto the bank's dry land. Max tried not to stare.

"Hello, Jinx. Who is your young friend?" Orville asked.

"Hello, Mr. Wright. This is Max. He's...uh...special, like me. He's a time traveler, too. We met last week, but I don't think it was by chance. Max, this is Mr. Orville Wright."

Max wiped his hands on his shorts and shook Orville's hand. "It's an honor to meet you, sir. Congratulations on your first flights. Jinx told me she got to witness them. Wow, that must have been so *awesome* for you!" He pumped Orville's hand up and down in his excitement. Petey ran in and around our legs, barking for joy.

Orville laughed and thanked Max. He reached down to pat Petey's head.

"It was awesome, as you said, Max. Will and I are still excited. It was quite the adventure–we were just the first lucky men to figure out the exact formula for flight."

The mist was heavy, now. It moved in and around us, wrapping us in a

curtain of fog that obscured our vision. I figured the moment to go had arrived.

"I guess you have something to show me, Mr. Wright. May Max and Petey come along?" I said. I grabbed Max's hand and hung on.

"Of course, Jinx. It's important for you both to see more, so you understand the whole story. This island contains so much of our early American history, concentrated right here on a stretch of land only 8 miles long by 2 miles wide. Extraordinary, when you think of it," said Orville.

Max and I slowly nodded, thinking about the truth to Orville's words. I swallowed hard. "Yes, sir, we're ready. Max, are you sure you want to do this?" He nodded and gave me a look that said: *Are you crazy? Try to leave me behind!*

"Pick up Petey, Max, and rejoin hands. Jinx, if you grab my shirttail and hang on, that should do it. Stay close by me when we get there. It

isn't time for you to interact with these people while in the past. That will come to you later. You will be observers. Are you ready?" said Orville.

Roanoke Island, 1587

The fog swirled around us in an ever-faster circle until we heard a great rushing sound, and the daylight dimmed until it blinked out. It felt like a giant vacuum cleaner sucked me into its tube, and we spiraled through space and time until we were dumped onto a beach on a sunny day. Max and I sat on the ground with the breath knocked out of us, while Petey did a jig around us. Orville stood nearby, smiling.

"None the worse for the trip, I hope," Orville said, in a low voice. "The landings will get better with time, I believe. Come along. They won't be able to see you, but we'll still be as quiet as possible. You know how sometimes you feel like you are being watched? That's how they might feel if we get too close. Follow me. We have a short way to walk."

We heard the people before we saw them, pounding, sawing, and chattering. Men, women, boys, and girls worked feverishly all around us. The men and boys wore loose fitted shirts and pants that came to their knees, with leather boots or shoes. Girls dressed as their mothers did in long skirts and dresses, aprons and scarves or bonnets covered their hair. There was no brightly colored clothing, rather muted browns and blues.

The adults all attended to jobs important for their immediate survival, like building the houses, cooking soups in big black kettles over open campfires, or driving large saplings into the ground to reform the walls of the fort that had fallen. The fort had an interesting shape–basically a square with arrowhead points on three sides.

Even the children had jobs; they carried tools to the men, searched for kindling, picked berries and nuts, all within sight of the adults.

"We're at Fort Raleigh, with the colonists, aren't we?" I asked.

Orville nodded his head. "Yes, notice how much they've got to do. They need shelters for each family. The fort had mostly been destroyed after Ralph Lane and his men gave up a year ago and sailed home on Sir Francis Drake's ship, that had stopped to check on them. Ralph Lane left fifteen men to watch the fort. Those were the men John White was supposed to pick up the next summer. Remember, they found the one skeleton, but no sign of the others? Indians told them the other men got into their boat and sailed away. But no one ever saw them again. So they were actually the first of the Lost Colonists.

"Now, though, Manteo and his tribe have promised to help the colonists through their first fall and winter. It is already August, too late for the colonists to plant seed for crops to mature into food," Orville said.

"Do they have supplies of food from the ships?" Max asked.

"Not much was left after the six week voyage. They will only have what they've managed to hunt or fish for," Orville said. "They are not prepared at all to face the hardships of winter. Most of these men are of the yeomanry class back in England–the farmers, tradesmen, and craft workers. They really don't know how to hunt and fish. Manteo's people can only give a small amount of food from their supplies. They weren't expecting over a hundred guests for the winter."

"Hmm..., things aren't going very well with the Indians, either," Max said. "I've witnessed some terrible attacks on the Indian villages that happened when Ralph Lane and his soldiers were first here. His soldiers raided villages, killed the Indians, and burnt their crops and fields. That certainly doesn't make it easy for these settlers." Max's eyes flashed anger.

Orville nodded. "That is exactly right, Max. Now, some of the Indians have become enemies. I wanted to help you both understood what these folks were up against."

Just then, I saw the leader, John White, come from the back of the fort. I recognized him from that vision I had when I was aboard their ship, weeks ago.

"Has anyone seen George Howe?" he asked. The men paused in their hammering and looked at each other.

"Yes, but he's been gone awhile, now," one man answered. "He said he was going crabbing."

"He went alone?" John asked. "Even though we haven't had any trouble with the Indians so far, it's important not to let down our guard. Remember my request that no one go anywhere without a partner? A few of you come with me. We'd best find him."

I felt my stomach rise up into my throat. This was not going to end well. I tugged Max's arm. "Max, maybe we shouldn't go with them. I have a bad feeling about this," I said.

Max looked grim. His face had an ashen color. "You stay here by the fort. I'll go."

I didn't want to lose sight of him, and Orville was nowhere to be found. He kept disappearing like that, I guess to let us experience things for ourselves. The idea of being left completely alone was worse than going along with Max, so, hugging Petey to my chest, I slowly walked behind him and the group of men.

We followed them down a tiny path through the reeds to the water. The men looked around, but there was no George Howe. They spread out to search.

Finally someone shouted, "Oh, no! Come quickly. He's over here".

I knew what to expect. Max tried to hold me back, but I wrenched my arm from his grip and followed the men.

There he laid, face down and floating in the water. He had arrows in his bare back. I felt faint. Max grabbed my arm again and walked me back up the path, away from the scene. We went to stand with Orville, who waited at the corner of the fort.

"Now what," I asked. "Will the colonists retaliate? And how will they know what tribe of Indians is responsible for killing Mr. Howe? It seems like the colonists and Indians are already into a spiral of fighting back and forth for awful deeds that were done to each other."

Orville nodded. "And so it begins," he said.

I knew what he meant. Petey whined at my feet. I stooped to pick him up again and buried my face in his soft fur.

John White and the other men came back to the fort area, carrying George Howe's body. They carefully laid him on the porch of one of the small cabins that had been finished. Everyone gathered around.

John bowed his head and said a quiet prayer. Then he addressed his group.

"We must not let this detain us from preparing our homes and gathering food for the winter. It's even more important to rebuild the shelter of the fort. When Ferdinando leaves us behind, we will send word with him back to England that we need shiploads of supplies. Roger Bailie and Ananias Dare will prepare

lists of food, seeds to plant, tools and other items that we require. Please see them if you have requests. Now, let us continue in our work, while the women prepare Mr. Howe's body for burial."

Mothers held their children close. I saw John White's daughter, Eleanor, still expecting her baby, protecting her swollen stomach within her folded arms. I wondered if she was the one I saw, hurrying through the woods with the little girl. The view I had of them had been so soft and faded that I wasn't sure. I checked around, through the group of huddled people, to see if I could spot the little girl who came to me on my first night at the beach. One, two, three...I counted nine boys. Over there, with another woman was a little girl, the only girl in the group. She wasn't the girl child I had seen in either vision, I felt sure about that. Hmmm...? I wondered.

The men and boys went back to their building projects, but I could see them exchange glances and look out beyond the fort area—to watch for the Indians. There was no more lively chatter or singing. The mood at the fort had turned from happy to somber and frightened. I just shook my head.

"Max, I can't imagine doing this, especially coming here with children, or expecting to have a baby. It's so dangerous for them all," I said.

"They were brave, that's for sure," Max said. He looked grim.

We both glanced at Orville, waiting for him to give his opinion. But he looked off into the woods, deep in thought.

Then he turned to us and said, "Come, Jinx and Max, enough for now. I'll return you to your home."

We had barely grabbed Petey and touched Orville's shirttail when that dark tunnel inhaled us and swirled us up through time. The trip was a fast, cold, blackout journey, but not quite as scary now.

Our landing was softer. We found ourselves perched on a log, near the rubber boat, while the light turned back on like someone had flopped a switch. Orville was gone. Sun, lapping water, the call of the sea birds, we were home again. But for how long?

Max and I looked around at the edge of the sound water flowing gently in to the shore. I wondered if Max pictured George Howe's poor body, bobbing in the water, riddled with arrows. At that moment, no matter how serene our surroundings were, the dead body was the only picture I could see.

Chapter Thirteen:

The Story of the Lost Colony–Part 2

Max's stitches were out, and his head wound healed quickly in the salt water of the ocean. His dad took us to the ocean beach again, so Max could continue my surfing lessons. Today, I actually got to my feet, crouched on the surfboard for the first time, and was able to ride a small wave in to the beach.

Petey leaped all around me when I jumped off the board onto the pebbles at the edge of our beach. *"Good job, Jinx, yeah! Take me out, take me out!"* Petey begged.

He rode a few waves in with Max, crouching surefooted, shaking off the saltwater when he jumped off the board. I felt very proud of my improving skills, and I was awed by Petey's natural surfing ability. What a great day of fun in the sun.

That night we had a roaring fire going again. Mom joined us, wearing jeans and a yellow sweater. She was finally going to finish the story of the Lost Colony.

We roasted marshmallows until they turned brown and gooey and watched the sun set in brilliant swirls of rosy colors. The burning wood smoke drifted upward and filled the air with a pleasant aroma of pine.

Max and I sat on the soft sand and leaned back against the log seat. We both wore shorts and tee shirts from Jockey's Ridge State Park. Our tanned legs stretched toward the fire, and I could feel the heat right through my toes and up into my tired legs. It felt good. Surfing was hard work. I pulled my Phillies sweatshirt on over my head. Petey lay between us. I stroked his velvety ears over and over.

"Are you all ready to hear the ending of the Lost Colony story?" Mom finally asked.

We nodded, but Max stiffened and looked at my mom. He wanted to share his newest vision about Wanchese and Manteo, but didn't seem to know where to start.

Max took a deep breath and pushed the shock of blond hair up off of his forehead. "I saw...when I was back in time...I felt like I was Wanchese, Mrs. MacKenzie. It felt like I...uh...slid into his body and could see and hear everything he experienced. Wanchese and Manteo were blood brothers for a long time, but they had a falling out over their views about the white people coming here to settle in a colony," he blurted out.

Mom wasn't surprised by what he said. She and Max's parents had shared worried concerns, about the new powers we were both developing. Everyone agreed that the misty air of Roanoke seemed to be the trigger that opened the floodgates to our new talents.

"That's right, Max. Why do you think you're seeing this history through the eyes of John White and Wanchese?" Mom asked.

"Er...well, these visions are giving Jinx and me a lot of historical background into the English attempts to colonize, and the Native Americans' reactions to them coming into their lives." Max said. "But instead of reading about it, I'm able to see it through a real person's eyes. It makes history become real. I think that I'm seeing things from the Indians' point of view, and Jinx is learning about the colonists' point of view. Right, Jinx?"

"That's for sure, Max," I said. "We're learning our history through seeing the people actually experience it as it happened. It really ties us to them and makes us feel all of their emotions. But we shouldn't judge either side, should we, Mom?"

"No, it's not for us to judge. Understanding both viewpoints helps us to think about what we would do in a similar situation, doesn't it?" Mom said.

Max and I nodded. I could tell we both remembered our latest trip to Fort Raleigh with Orville to see how hard the colonists had to work for survival. We also knew how the Indians felt about the settlers when George Howe's body was found floating in the sound, shot full of arrows.

"I'd like to hear about what happened next, Mom," I said. I was anxious to hear the rest of this mysterious story. For the first time in my life, I felt the ties that bound me to the past.

Mom leaned forward and put her arms on her knees. She began in her soft voice.

"The colonists made the best of a bad situation by throwing themselves into preparing homes for the winter. It was already late August...

Roanoke Island–Autumn, 1587

As can be imagined, the colonists had many mixed feelings that summer; anxiety about surviving the winter having had no planting time, and great fear of being attacked by angry Indians.

One of the few happy occasions they had was the birth of Governor White's granddaughter, Virginia Dare, on August 18th, 1587. The first white child to be born in America, she gave them a reason for celebration. This small baby girl brought hope and light to their hard days. They held the celebration on August 24th, after baby Virginia was baptized into the Church of England. Baby Virginia and Manteo, Lord of Roanoke, held the honor of being the first two recorded baptisms into the Church of England in North America.

The colonists' relations with the once friendly Roanoac Indians really deteriorated when Wanchese and Manteo broke off their friendship. The Roanoacs no longer trusted these white men who did not keep their word.

The earlier English explorers had stolen from them, burned their crops of corn, and even killed many of their people, including their head weroance, Wingina. How could these people be any different, they thought.

As Captain Ferdinando and his ship Lyon finished unloading the ships supplies and prepared to return to England, the villagers called a meeting with Governor White. A spokesman delivered the message as they all gathered around the smoky campfire in the center of the fort. John White looked around at the solemn faces of his colonists.

Ananias spoke to his father-in-law. "We need many more tools and provisions to be able to plant and hunt in this wilderness. We fear for our survival. So, we voted for you and another leader to return to England on board the Lyon to get supplies. If you leave now, you should be back by springtime. Manteo and his people will help us with hunting and food this winter. We hope to be able to get through 'til spring."

Governor White shook his head and put his palms up, as if to ward off this dangerous suggestion. "I could never desert you, my brave friends. Please, do not ask this of me. I am your appointed leader. We can send two of my trusted assistants to obtain these supplies for us," Governor White pleaded.

"But you are the most important, being our Governor. Your word of our needs will bear the heaviest weight upon Sir Walter Raleigh and the Queen," Ananias said.

After many attempts of trying to convince John White to go on their behalf, he finally broke down and agreed. He prepared to sail with Ferdinando and the Lyon on the next high tide.

John White called the villagers together before his departure. He had been worrying day and night about the fate of his colony while he would be gone.

"We need to work out a method for you to communicate your new location if an attack by the Spanish privateers or the Indians cause need to flee," John declared.

One of the villagers had an idea. "We will carve the name of the new location onto a tree if we must move elsewhere. If it is because of danger, we will add a carving of the Maltese cross as a distress signal."

They all knew the symbol of the Maltese cross. The points of the cross symbolized the eight points of courage: loyalty, piety, bravery, generosity, contempt of death, glory and honor, helpfulness towards the sick, and respect for church These were worthy goals for the colonists to remember.

With these plans laid, Governor White said a tearful goodbye to the small band of people. He gave his daughter, Eleanor, a close hug and rocked his infant granddaughter gently in his arms one last time. Virginia waved her tiny fists and kicked her legs, causing them all to smile through the tears.

John pressed a package into his daughter's hands. "For my precious grand-daughter Virginia, when she is old enough," he said.

"God speed, Father. Our undying love sails with you," Eleanor said, "and I pray your speedy and safe return to us." She held on to her father, afraid to let him go.

John gently pulled back from his daughter's embrace. "God be with you all," he replied, as he looked out over the sea of hopeful and trusting faces, then forced the thought of not seeing them again his mind.

The colonists waved from the shore of Roanoke Island, long after it was possible for the men on board the Lyon to see them. With hopeful spirits, they started back through the wooded area to the security of the fort.

Only Eleanor, embracing the mysterious package and Baby Virginia tightly to her chest, stood on the beach for a long while that morning. She watched the sails of the flagship Lyon and her flotilla of smaller ships disappear from sight while tears slid down her checks.

England, Autumn 1587– Spring 1588

When Governor White reached England aboard the Lyon that fall, he found his homeland in a frenzy of prewar tension. Spain had threatened to attack England, and word reached England that a mighty Spanish armada of warships was being gathered. England immediately canceled all expeditions and called every ship into service for Her Majesty, the Queen.

John first visited the benefactor of the Roanoke colony. "Please, Sir Walter," John White begged, "Our colonists on Roanoke Island need help with supplies. I must make haste to return to them."

Sir Walter was firm in his response. "Nay sir. That will not happen. Even good men with righteous causes must make sacrifices. England's fate relies on the defense our ships will provide against the Spanish Armada. The Queen requested all English ships be pressed into service, and we will obey the Queen."

Governor White was quick with his reply. "And our colonists in America depend on supply ships for their survival. This was your dream, Sir Walter, to plant an English colony in the Americas. Now will you desert them in their time of trouble?"

Sir Walter bowed his head in thought. The impending war with Spain was horrible timing to send help for the colony. "Very well, then, I'll see what I can manage to do. There may be a slight chance of sending two supply ships." But it was to be months before he could find and free ships to send to the colony in America.

April 22nd, 1588, two supply ships left the port in England, only three months ahead of the fearsome Spanish Armada attack. This was the beginning of a run of bad luck for Governor White. With White aboard the ship named Brave, the two ships got into a fight with the French at sea.

White recorded in his journal that the large French warships quickly overtook the Brave and threw grappling hooks, so their men could board to fight. In hand-to-hand combat, White was wounded twice in the head and shot in the side of his buttock. They were looted by the French man-o-war and set adrift.

The sailors who survived had to mend and repair the sails and tackle before they could limp back to England. Governor John White was bitterly disappointed by the failure to return to his colony and family stranded in America.

The Attack of the Spanish Armada, England–1588

John White remained frantic. The thought of his family and the other colonists never left his mind. He tried again to arrange meetings with Sir Richard Grenville and Sir Walter Raleigh to discuss returning to America, but they had other more important business at hand. By now news reached England that the mighty Spanish Armada was nearing the English Channel, ready to attack.

King Philip II of Spain had sent a fleet of one hundred thirty ships, with twenty-two outfitted as fighting galleons. They sailed into the English Channel in a crescent shape, with the fighting ships inside the crescent, protected by the faster, smaller boats around them.

The English were prepared to fight. When the Armada was spotted, beacons were lit as signals along the coastline, quickly spreading their warning light all the way to London.

When news reached Sir Francis Drake, he was in the midst of playing a game of bowls. He replied that he had plenty of time to finish his game. Drake had a brilliant plan. He had eight old ships loaded up with anything that would burn well. The floating bombs were lit and set adrift during the night for the currents to carry them into the resting Armada.

The Spanish soldiers knew about the floating firebombs, but could do little about them, as they were trapped in the channel by English ships that had cut off their escape. They also knew their own ships were loaded with ammunition that would light up and explode. So they broke out of their protective crescent shape and tried to sail free of the fire ships.

There was little space to maneuver in the channel and the winds were not cooperating. The English firebombs swept down on top of the helpless Spanish galleons. The first Spanish fighting galleon exploded like fireworks when it was hit, and many others were quickly set afire. Explosions ripped through the air, over and over. This was a complete disaster for the so-called mighty Spanish Armada.

The Spanish were able to hold off some attacks by the British, but their food and water supplies dwindled. Soldiers had to eat rope for survival. Vicious storms hit them and damaged many of their ships. When they tried to sail around Ireland to ask for help, the Irish attacked them. Many of the surviving sailors began to die of diseases like scurvy, dysentery and high fevers.

King Philip's great Spanish Armada had to admit defeat and return home. Only about sixty-seven ships out of one hundred and thirty returned to Spain. Over twenty thousand Spanish soldiers and sailors were killed or died of disease.

The English lost no ships and only about one hundred men in battle. However, disease did claim over seven thousand English soldiers and sailors, also.

So, in the end, England's streamlined ships did indeed whip Spain's large, cumbersome galleons and sent them packing back to Spain.

Roanoke Island, America–August 18, 1590

After the war, John White finally had his transportation arranged to go back to America. But these were not supply ships; they were four privateer ships hoping to capture Spanish galleons loaded with treasure headed back home to Spain. The privateers had only agreed to drop John off at Roanoke Island. White hoped that supply ships would arrive soon after he reached Roanoke Island.

Once again approaching the Outer Banks off the coast of America, John White's heart seemed to be in his throat, and he could scarcely contain his excitement and apprehension. It had been two years and seven months since he left his beloved family and the colonists on Roanoke Island. They had been long, dangerous, and frustrating years. Now he finally made good on his promise to return to the colony–but without the much-needed supplies.

When they first arrived in the area of Roanoke Island, the ships' captains continued to roam the coast for weeks in hopes of robbing and looting Spanish ships for their supplies. Then, fierce and damaging storms tossed them around like toy boats until everyone feared for their lives. All of this continued to frustrate Governor White.

Even with this many problems, John White never gave up hope of returning to his colony. They finally dropped anchor at Roanoke Island on the exact date of his granddaughter Virginia's third birthday, August 18th. He would finally see her and be with her to celebrate her birthday, God willing. As he looked toward the land, he saw smoke drifting into the air.

"Ahoy. Look yonder," he shouted, "I think I see the welcoming smoke near the place where I left our Colony. I have great hope that it is a sign from the colonists expecting my return."

"Step lively, Mates," the captain of the good ship Hopewell briskly ordered. "Load and fire the canons as greeting to let them know that we have returned." The cannons roared an announcement of their arrival. But no one came to the beach to wave a welcome.

After landing, the men found the first sign of trouble on a tree near the beach.

White dashed over to the tree. "Men, look here! The Roman letters, C-R-O, are carved into the bark, according to the plan we made if they needed to go to a new location," said John White. "I think they traveled inland, fifty miles or so, to Croatoan, near Cape Hatteras. They must be safe with Manteo and his people."

He was anxious to get to the fort to find other clues. "Follow me. I know the way to the Fort Raleigh," White yelled. However, the path was badly overgrown with tangled brush and vines. The men hacked their way through and finally reached the fort.

It was obvious that Fort Raleigh had been abandoned for some time. It, too, was overgrown with tall grasses and weeds and pumpkin vines gone wild. Heavy iron bars, pots, and pans lay scattered in disarray.

The men also found the remains of five heavy chests of goods and items that had been carefully hidden by the colonists in an old trench. But they had been dug up and looted, probably by the Indians. Broken furniture and other household items lay in ruins. Even John White's art supplies and personal items that he had left behind had been stolen.

White spotted a second sign behind the fort. "Here, another carving on a tree!"

The bark had been removed about five feet high from the ground. Letters had been cut into the smooth surface. "This time there are the letters spelling out the whole word," he said. John rubbed his hand over the rough-cut letters, almost as if for good luck.

CROATOAN

"There is no sign of a Maltese cross carved for danger. I know they shall be found safe," John added. Saying this aloud will make it so, he thought

Doubts about his colony's safety continued to creep into John's mind. He angrily pushed them away. In their searches, they had found no skeletons, burial grounds, or any sign of the colonists, which still gave him hope of their survival.

With no reason to stay on Roanoke Island, John White made plans to go inland to Croatoan. "The smoke that we saw–it must have been from the coastal Indian village of the Croatoans. They are Manteo's people. Please, we must go inland. I know they'll welcome us," he told the captain.

"I can only spare a few days to check inland with the Indians. We have other important business for the Queen. Who knows where the colonists could have gone, or what happened to them. It's been years, White," the Captain said.

His bad luck continued, and those plans to go inland never came about. That same day fearsome storms hit the coast again. The two ships that had traveled together, the Hopewell and the Moonlight, were forced to go further off coast to drop anchor, hoping to ride out the storms. The giant waves pitched and rolled in the howling wind and tossed and buffeted the small ships. The superstitious sailors believed all the fearsome monsters of the deep were attacking them.

Anchor cables snapped over and over while the men frantically tied new anchors to drop. The ships drifted closer to the dangerous, jagged rocks on the coast. Sailors were accidentally killed while trying to save the ships. Captain Spicer, of the good ship Moonlight, and six of his brave seamen drowned. That final, terrible accident broke the sailors' morale. The terrified sailors refused to keep at the task of heading for Croatoan, and the Hopewell and Moonlight turned tail and set sail for home.

John White, would-be Governor of the City of Raleigh, lost all hope of ever seeing his family and the colonists alive again.

No word of their well being ever reached him. Even though later colonists from Jamestown searched for the missing colonists and questioned the Indians, the Roanoke colony was never located. Ninety-one men, seventeen women, and nine children all disappeared into the mist. To this day they are known as Sir Walter Raleigh's Lost Colony.

Mom's voice dropped off in silence. Max and I shivered in the chill and dampness of the evening and unconsciously scooted towards the fire, until our shoulders touched for comfort.

"Mom, that's the best history mystery I've ever heard. It gives me Goosebumps!"

"Yeah, Mrs. MacKenzie, you made it come alive," said Max. "When I was John White, or, um...when he...when I witnessed those attacks on Wingina's village through his eyes, I knew in my heart that it would cause dangerous problems between colonists and the Native Americans. Maybe they attacked the fort?"

It was still difficult for Max to explain how he seemed to become a person from the past and see through their eyes. Max rubbed the back of his head, where his stitches had been.

Mom sighed and tilted her head, looking out across the sound at the lights from the other islands. We sat in silence for a while. Petey had crept into Max's lap to comfort him.

Finally, Mom said, "So Jinx, I thought you might want to research more about the Lost Colony for your paper. Maybe you and Max will be able to figure out what happened to those poor, lost souls."

No question about it. I was definitely hooked on the story of the Lost Colony. And I sure wanted to figure out the mystery of the little ghost girl. We had already learned so much from our visions and trips to the past. I wanted to dig into more research on my laptop right now, but it was late in the evening.

Mom stood up, stretched, and gave a big yawn. "I'm beat. I'll leave you two alone to make your plans for tomorrow. The fire's almost out, but please throw some sand on it before you come back to the cottage."

She turned to go, stopped, and tilted her head again, looking back toward the woods. Her brow wrinkled, and she looked and puzzled as she checked the area. Then she smiled back at us.

"Jinx, don't be too much longer. It's probably time for us all to be in for the night, safe and sound."

Max and I gazed into the glowing embers of the fire in silence and mulled over the story Mom had just finished. Petey now snuggled securely in my lap and slept.

"Max, I'm convinced the little colonial girl is from the Lost Colony. She may be able to give us some hints about what happened. All I have to do is be brave enough to communicate with her."

Before Max could comment, Petey jumped out of my lap and stood quivering in the sand. His ears alert, he looked back toward the woods.

"A white doe. She's beautiful," Petey told us.

A soft, gray mist swirled around an outcropping of moss-covered boulders at the edge of the woods. The whole area seemed to brighten, as if highlighted with a soft, white spotlight.

Very delicately, from behind the rocks stepped a pure snow-white deer. There was not a spot of color on her. She took a few steps onto the sand and paused facing us, with one front leg bent and frozen in the air. She would flee at one little sound. We didn't dare breath. Her dark eyes watched us with interest for a few seconds. She turned to go, then looked back at us and seemed to beckon with a twist of her head. The soft light surrounding her slowly dimmed. The white doe vanished from our sight ino the mist.

I heard Max expel a big breath of air. Petey turned to us, wagging his whole body in excitement.

"Nice deer, the white doe. She's a friend. I think she needs help, too."

"Did I mention to you that Petey makes friends with every ghost he runs into, human or animal?" I telecommunicated to Max.

"No, you did not," Max sent back, *"and I'll thank you to remember to tell your partner important things like that. Now let's go, let's get outta here. We'll deal with that spooktacular event tomorrow!"*

We doused the embers and scrambled back over the dunes to our safe cottages without another word.

Chapter Fourteen:

Hot On the Trail

The next morning, Max showed up early. And, okay, so maybe I was a bit grumpy, but it was only 7:30 in the morning, and I'd just spent a terrible night. I'd tossed and turned, unable to shut down my brain. I had rehashed all the Big Mystery events of the last few days.

"Add the white ghost deer to the list," I griped to Petey. "What on earth was that all about? Now we have one more thing to worry about and figure out."

"Jinx needs to have breakfast. You're grouchy." Petey said.

Petey disappeared downstairs and returned with his bowl. He dumped his dog food all over my quilt. I guess he was trying to make me feel better. I had to laugh at him. His furry clown face was so cute.

"Oh Pete-o, that is very kind of you, but I think I prefer people food this morning."

His look said I didn't know what good food was.

"Hey Jinx. Rise and shine. We've got research to do," Max shouted up the stairs. "You have five minutes before I run up there and drag you out by the heels."

"Yeah, you and who else?" I shouted back, as I jumped out of bed and ran to the bathroom to wash my face and try to tame my crazy hair. It looked so bad that I almost scared myself when I looked in the mirror. Bad hair day. Oh, well. I jumped into my blue shorts, pulled a pale blue cotton tee shirt over my head, and ran barefoot down the steps. Petey, ever faithful, ran by my side.

Max sat at the kitchen table, already munching on peanut butter and jelly toast and sipping hot chocolate. He jumped to his feet and flipped a dishtowel over his arm. He bowed as he said, "Good morning, Madame. I am Max, your server. What may I bring you theeeese beau-tee-ful morning? May I recommend zee hot choc-o-late? It eese made with zee finest cocoa beans of zee Caribbean."

"You know, I can't stand morning people," I commented. But we both laughed.

He looked calm, rested, and ready for action. He had on a clean pair of khaki shorts and a beat up, comfortable looking "Go Navy" sweatshirt.

We plopped down and continued our breakfast.

"Your mom just left," Max said. "She'll be back in a few hours to see if we need help with the research. She'll be at the archeological dig site."

"Yeah, that's her summer project, to work at the dig," I said. "I think they're sifting the dirt around the historic areas, looking for early colonial-era artifacts. I never thought I'd say this, but I'm actually anxious to start researching the Lost Colony. We might find some good clues to help us solve the Big Mystery."

Max's eyes shone with excitement. "You know, meeting you was the best thing that ever happened to me," he said. All of a sudden, he sort of got tongue-tied. He reached up to fiddle with that one curl of hair that always wrapped around behind his left ear. "I... I feel honored to work with such a talented, nice girl...um, you know what I mean? You're special, different."

His voice trailed off and we locked eyes for a long moment before he shifted his gaze and coughed in embarrassment.

"Thanks Max. That's the nicest thing a boy ever said to me."

Omigosh! I think he likes me. You know...in a girlfriend-boyfriend kinda way. I looked at the ceiling–huh! There was a cobweb up there in the corner. *Okay, okay, okay.* I took a deep breath to steady myself. *We have stuff to do, so move on Jinx,* I told myself.

Max continued, "Seeing that white ghost deer was really an awesome experience last night, although it did kind of scare me silly. These strange things happened for a purpose, I know they're all related. I plan to search for clues about the white deer, for starters."

"Good idea. I'll look for clues about what may have happened to the Lost Colony."

We washed our mugs and plates and set up a workstation for our computers. I dragged out a box of supplies.

"You have to love the twenty-first century," I told Max and Petey. "It should be a law that every kid gets a free lap-top and Internet access." We collected notebooks, pens, and pencils from the box. We were ready to roll.

"All right, let's surf and take notes for about an hour. Then we'll take a break and share what we've found," said Max.

He furiously tapped on his keyboard and soon was deep into reading.

Ok, I thought, *jump in.* I sat and stared at the computer. *Hmmm... where to start?* I flexed my fingers and typed "Roanoke Island" into the search engine and immediately got a bunch of hits. Most sites talked about the island as the resort and listed all of the fun vacation things to do.

Let's try another way, I thought. I punched in "The Lost Colony" and the screen filled with what seemed like a million web sites. It overwhelmed me. I'm not very good at making choices, so I sat and stared for a long time.

Petey finally came over to me and placed his front paws up on my arm. He looked at the screen, tapped the mouse with his right paw and scrolled down. Then he gave a final tap and opened up a site. He gave me a stern look, and said, *"Jinx, get going."*

I laughed and saluted him. "Aye, Aye, Captain Salty Old Sea Dog." He had picked a good one, and I soon began to scribble notes.

Hours later, Max and I came out of our research trance and looked at each other, amazed to see how much time had passed.

"I found great stuff, Max. There are lots of clues from journal entries of the Jamestown Colony leaders. I also found a neat legend handed down, that tells a story of what may have happened to the Lost Colony."

"Good job, ace detective. I hit gold, too. Wait until you hear this *Legend of the White Doe,*" Max said. We both looked at each other. I knew we were both thinking about our white doe in the mist.

"I'm starved. Let's grab some sandwiches. I'll go first with the debriefing," I offered.

"Sounds good to me. Debriefing? You're really starting to sound like the head of the *JMP History Mystery Detective Agency,* now."

We made some tuna fish sandwiches, grabbed some carrots and grapes, and headed out for the porch swing on the back deck. Some ominous looking black thunderheads had formed in the south, but the sky over us was sunny and blue.

"What's for dessert?" asked Max.

I picked up the bowl of grapes and waved it in the air, my cheeks stuffed full of tuna sandwich.

"Oh come on," Max said. "I need something better than that. We need energy." He picked up his backpack and pulled out two huge peanut butter chocolate bars.

"All right," I cheered. "Mom seldom has any good junk food around."

Petey gobbled a few dog biscuits and ran off to the dunes to explore.

"Stay in sight, Fur Face," I told him.

He gave me a wag of his tail. He had a habit of going off exploring on his own, and I always worried about him.

While we finished our lunch, I started to tell Max about some of the clues I found.

"There's such confusion," I said, "and so many different ideas floating around. "A lot of what we know today was written in the journals of the early Jamestown Colony leaders. Most of that was what they heard, not actually witnessed. The Lost Colony was founded in 1587 and went missing by 1590, right?"

Max nodded in agreement while he crunched a carrot, so I continued.

"Jamestown colony had thrived by the early 1600's. Okay, so here's Clue 1. One of the leaders, George Percy, organized an expedition to search for the lost colonists further up the James River. He wrote that they spotted a savage boy among the Indians with a head of perfectly yellow hair, and his skin was much whiter than the Natives."

"Listen to you," said Max. He leaned back in his chair and cocked his head to the side. "You're really sounding like a history nut, spouting out all of those dates. What else have you got?"

"It's not nice to call your friend a nut," I said, and rolled my eyes.

Secretly, I was proud of myself for finding such important clues.

"Ok, Clue 2," I continued on. "A later Jamestown leader, Captain John Smith, wrote that he talked with Indian chiefs who reported seeing white men dressed like the colonists further inland. He heard they lived in English-style houses."

"This is getting pretty good," Max said. Those are great clues about what might have happened to the lost colonists.

"Ahem, please listen to Clue 3. Jamestown sent men out to search–again. They wrote that they actually talked to these Indians who said they saw white men, but the Indians wouldn't take them to the white people."

"Wow," said Max. "Wonder why not? Do you think the Native Americans were afraid Jamestown soldiers would attack their village?"

"Maybe. With all those horrible attacks against the Indian villages that you witnessed, do you blame them for being secretive? And finally, Clue 4 is presented," I said proudly. "The Indians denied access to the search party, but the soldiers wrote that they found fresh carvings on trees in the area. Guess what? The trees had crosses and Christian messages carved there. Things only the colonists would have known about."

As we thought these clues over, Max finally said, "So what do you deduce, partner?"

I answered carefully as an idea formed in my head. "Well, since Jamestown was the first successful colony right after the Lost Colony, I think those reports of white men being spotted had to be the lost colonists. I think they did survive and lived inland among the other friendly tribes, probably the Croatoans first, then maybe others."

"Yeah. That makes sense." Max said. "And since historians accept Christopher Columbus' journal from the 1400s as accurate, I think these 1600s Jamestown journals must be pretty accurate, too. Jinx, we're hot on the trail."

He stopped and tugged on his hair. "But, I still don't understand why they moved when they expected Governor John White to return with supplies"

"I think you and I both have ideas on that," I said. I flopped back in my chair. "My head is swirling with information overload. Do you want to go swimming? We've worked hard enough for one summer day. We could have another campfire meeting tonight to share the legends we found."

"Sounds good to me," Max said. He was already headed for the dunes.

Loud woofs and piercing screams of angry gulls disturbed the afternoon peace. Petey flew over the dunes, with his tail tucked under and his ears laid back along his furry head.

Petey barked, *"Help, SOS! Gulls are mad. Just sniffing their nests wouldn't hurt them."*

"Oh no," said Max. "Petey rescues are becoming a habit."

We chased the gulls and shooed them away with our beach towels, while Petey dived for cover under the deck.

Chapter Fifteen:

More Clues

The campfire blazed once more. The sunset had been exceptionally pretty because dark clouds gathered on the horizon. As the sun sank lower, it had backlit the towering cumulonimbus clouds in vivid oranges and reds. Now, in the soft darkness, we settled around the fire.

Mom joined us to hear about our progress, and we all made sticky, gooey S'mores.

Petey blatantly begged for treats. *"I love S'mores! I love them! Please, please, please?"* He flipped in the air.

"No chocolate for you Petey," I said. "Caffeine is bad for little doggie hearts."

"Awww, let him have a marshmallow at least," said Max. He tossed a couple to Petey.

"Holy Mackerel! Only one," I said. "Just what we need–more sugar for our hyper active little Jack Russell buddy. If he doesn't calm down to sleep tonight, I'm sending him over to you." Petey snatched the marshmallows up before I could grab them and dashed out of my reach. It was obvious he was delighted.

Mom laughed at us. "It sounds like you two head honchos from the *JMP History Mystery Detective Agency* are making fast progress on the Lost Colony mystery."

I gave her a shocked look. "How do you know about our club? I didn't tell you."

"Oh, let's just say moms make it their responsibility to know what's going on. Let's hear the legend that you found, Jinx. So you think you know why the colonists moved on before John White returned from England?"

"Yes, I do," I nodded. "Ok, walk this way, History Fans," I said, in my best "Mom story-telling" voice. "It was a dark and stormy night..."

"Oh, no." Max pretended to hit his forehead with his open palm. "You two are clones."

"Quiet, detective, let me begin..."

The Legend of the Secret Cave

Chief Manteo's heart pounded with fear. He hurried silently through the woods and made his way back toward the village of the colonists on Roanoke Island. He had been away all day with some of his Croatoan tribesmen, to harvest fish from the ocean's bountiful waters. It had been a beautiful, peaceful day, when nothing occurred out of the ordinary until late afternoon. A messenger arrived at the shore. He waved his arms frantically to attract the fishermen's attention. Hostile Roanoac Indians had been spotted on the island. They talked of a plan to attack Fort Raleigh.

Chief Manteo respected these brave, white-skinned men and women who came so far from their native England to start new lives, and he had become a trusted advisor of Governor White. They were now his friends. So, he and his fishing party beached the canoes, and he urged the rest of the men to wait for his instructions.

Now, still a few miles away from the fort the fort, he slowed his pace, then crept closer and peered through the trees. Manteo's heart sank. He saw Chief Wanchese and his Roanoac war party were gathered and preparing to raid the colonists. He thought they would probably wait for nightfall. Their anger and hatred of the white men over losing their land and food had finally boiled over the edge.

"Hi-eeee, hiiii-eeeee..." War chants began to spill out of angry mouths.

Manteo heard their shrill war cries before their leader hushed them. Chief Wanchese wanted his braves to descend upon the small village of huts outside the fort like a swarm of angry wasps, with no warning.

Manteo felt deep sorrow that he and Wanchese had grown so far apart and were now enemies. He raced all the way to the fort on bare feet that were as silent as a breath of air.

He watched two of the guards who ran back to Fort Raleigh. They shouted news of the war party. "Indians! Indian attack coming! To the fort!"

Women scurried and children screamed and cried as the men yelled orders to run to the fort for safety. Once inside, they pulled the gates closed and pushed the wooden bars across the doors to lock them.

Manteo had to act quickly to save his white friends. If I can only get them from the fort through the secret tunnels to the cave, I can lead them to the waiting canoes on the beach. We still have a few hours of daylight. I hope the peaceful Croatoans in my village will take them in for protection, he thought.

He made his way through the tunnel that the colonists had dug and entered the fort. The men agreed with him–this time the Roanoac tribe meant to kill the men and probably take the women and children for slaves.

Ananias called for the colonists to be silent. "There is no time to take anything with us. We must hurry to save our lives. Women and children go first. Follow Manteo. Men, grab guns and ammunition and take up the rear."

Ananias could barely breathe. His chest felt so tight, there must surely be iron bands around it. I know the people need a strong leader–not someone who falls completely apart when faced with danger, he thought. But where are my wife, Eleanor, and my daughter, Virginia? They aren't inside the closed fort walls. I will send the others onward, but I must fall behind and go to search for my family. I will not desert them again. Not like my father-in-law, John White, has done. He felt angry and deserted by John White, himself.

The secret tunnel began inside the rear of the fort, went underground, and emptied into a small cavern near the banks of the sound. One by one, the colonists crawled in. Dirt spilled into their hair and eyes. They pushed deeper. It was hard to breathe. Hearts pounded, and they gasped for air. Finally, the women and children scrambled into the cave and spilled outside. They hurried to the Croatoan canoes. The tunnel was very tight for the bulkier men, but soon they broke through into the cave and then out into the bright sunlight, too.

Except one man did not follow the colonists' frantic quest for safety. Ananias Dare doubled back to the fort, hiding as best he could behind trees and brush, searching for his wife and child. Will I find them in time? I must not fail...

At nightfall, the Roanoke warriors crept through the woods. They moved like the silent creatures of the forest, without a crackle of leaves or snap of sticks in the brush.

At a signal, they attacked the fort. Iiiiii-eeeee...Iii-eee! Angry war screams filled the air. The warriors battered and hacked at the high stockade gates. They whooped and yelled. They would kill these white intruders and take all of their valuable food and supplies. This would send a message to the white men far away in England to stay in their own homeland. The Roanoacs' message would be that they did not want liars and thieves for their neighbors.

The gates gave way. The warriors swarmed inside and raced from back to front. Soon they began to mill about in confusion. There was not a white man, woman, or child to be found. The colonists had disappeared–right before their unbelieving eyes.

When I finished the legend, Max's eyes sparkled like the campfire's flames. He had an excited grin on his face.

"I know what you're thinking," he said. "Even though this was a legend, you believe this is the reason the colonists abandoned Roanoke Island, because of an attack by unfriendly Indians."

I nodded my head. "If we could find that tunnel and cave, we would lend some credibility to the theory that they had to escape an attack and went to live among Manteo's tribe," I said. "Just imagine, two kids actually finding some new evidence after four hundred years of searching." I sat forward. *"And we'd be those two kids."*

Max jumped to his feet, and he and Petey looked ready to tear off on a wild search that very moment.

"We've got some important hiking and searching to do during the next few days," he said. "I bet Petey's great sense of smell could track the scent of the tunnel."

"I can. I can. I know I can! Jinx, Max, let's go," Petey told us.

Petey jumped and wiggled in midair, because he was so excited.

A cold wind suddenly kicked in, and the flames flickered like crazy fingers. Lightning streaked across the dark sky. We heard low, rumbling thunder in the distance. As we all looked skyward, I saw clouds scudding over the moon.

"Now, wait just a minute, you three. I'm not exactly crazy about you crawling around in any ancient holes in the ground," Mom fretted. "Besides, this island structure couldn't support a system of tunnels and caves, anyway."

"Aw, Mom, c'mon! Use your imagination. Maybe the tunnel was a magical portal, like when Max shot into the time tunnel while surfing."

Mom gave me one of her I-can't-believe-you-just-said-that looks. "I *promise* we won't go anywhere dangerous–especially without an adult. I know the rules. We just want to scout around."

"Uh-huh. Well, I'm going to scout my way back to the cottage," Mom said.

She looked at the lightning flickering again in the distance.

"Did you hear the weather report for the next few days? They're watching a coastal low that's forming and have put the Outer Banks on storm watch," she told us.

"Oh no," Max said. "Our first bad storm of the summer. I hope it doesn't stop our search."

"Make sure you listen to the weather report in the morning for updates before you go traipsing off on any long jaunts," Mom said. "I'll say goodnight to you all. See you back at the cottage soon, Jinx?" She shivered as she glanced around. "It always seems to be a bit strange around here this time of night. Oh, well, must be the storms on the way."

It's more than the storms that are strange around here, I thought.

"We won't be long, Mom. Max wants to tell me one more legend about the Lost Colony that he found on the Internet today. Are you sure you don't want to hear it?"

"Thanks, but I'm on my way back to read the evening newspaper. Now don't forget to..."

"I know, I know, don't forget to douse the fire," I finished for her.

"You've got it, detectives," Mom said. With a little wave, she trotted back up over the dunes.

I watched her go back the path that led to home. *I love Mom, but she really doesn't have a sense of adventure,* I thought. I shook my head.

I turned back to Max with an eager smile.

"So what have you got? You said it's really good."

"Oh, yeah! Wait 'til you hear this one. It even goes along with your legend about Manteo saving the colonists. It's called 'The Legend of the White Doe.'"

Max paused for effect, and I gave a look over my shoulder at the boulders back near the tree line, where we had seen the white ghost deer last night.

"Walk this way, History Fans. It was a dark and stormy night..." Max started.

I just groaned, and he began his story.

The Legend of the White Doe

It was some years after the raid on the colonists at Fort Raleigh by the Roanoac tribe. They had barely escaped with their lives when Manteo led them inland to his village.

Near Manteo's village at Hatteras, a beautiful, fair-skinned, young maiden made her way to the sandy shores of a nearby beach. Her name was Virginia Dare. She had been a small child when Manteo rescued her colony from certain death at the hands of the angry Roanoacs. Her people had been adopted as brothers and sisters by the kind Croatoan tribe. Virginia loved them all equally, but was not nearly old enough to consider marriage. So she turned down many suitors.

Old Chico, who was the tribal medicine man, tried in vain to win her heart. Virginia kindly turned down his offers of marriage, also. Being furious with her, Chico vowed to himself that if he could not have her, no one would.

One night, by the light of the moon, Chico lifted his arms to the sea nymphs. "I ask you, oh mighty beings from the sea, help me with my plans. The young girl, Virginia, must be punished." Chico shook his rattles and sprinkled magic mixtures into the sound water. "Yes," the answer came to him. "We sea creatures will aid you." He smiled an evil smile and went home.

Virginia hurried on her way to meet her friend. She hummed a gentle English lullaby that her mother had taught her. She had received a message to meet her best friend, Fox Maiden, for a walk along the beach so they could gather clams for a feast to be held in the village.

She didn't know that Chico's secret plot was to kidnap her and take her back to Roanoke Island. He was the one who had sent the message to Virginia. Suddenly, her happy song turned to cries of fear as a huge, rank buckskin was thrown over her head from behind. She was tossed roughly onto the bottom of a dugout canoe.

Virginia cried out, "Please, who are you? Let me go, please..." But no one answered her cries for help.

When they reached the shores of her birthplace, Chico called upon the Sea Nymphs again, to help him with his revenge. He put the struggling young maiden onto the sand and removed the bearskin. He shook his rattles again and dusted Virginia with his magic potions. "Now you belong to the island. No one will marry you." Instead of Virginia, a snow-white doe struggled to her feet and ran off toward the woods.

Rumors of a magical, snow-white doe, leader of all the deer on Roanoke Island, began to be whispered among the Croatoans and the Roanoacs. Many young men hoped to hunt and slay this white deer so that prizes and honor would be bestowed upon them. But no-one's arrow ever seemed to be able to claim this creature.

One day Young Wanchese, son of Chief Wanchese of the Roanoacs, decided to try. His father had been presented with a magical, silver-tipped arrow from Queen Elizabeth upon his visit to England. Surely young Wanchese would be successful with such a powerful arrow. He stole the arrow when his father wasn't home and hid it among his own arrows. The white doe will be mine, this time I feel it, he thought.

Sure enough, on the day of the great hunt organized by his tribe, he was the first to spot the white deer. As the majestic white deer stepped out of the woods, he took careful aim. She turned and ran in fear, but the silver-tipped arrow found its mark. The snow-white doe fell to the ground, dying.

Young Wanchese ran triumphantly to his prey, but his joyful mood turned to horror. The White Doe mistily changed back into a young maiden. With her last breath, she whispered her name to him, "Virginia Dare."

It is said that the great spirit of the White Doe still roams in the mist of the island of Roanoke, searching for the way back to her people.

Ka-boom! We jumped as a crack of lightning lit up the beach like the flash of a giant camera.

"One thousand one, one thousand two, one thousand three..." I counted, before the thunder rumbled closer. "The storm's only about three miles away. It's moving fast.

I turned to Max. "Wow! That was some trick you did with the crack of lightning as a great finale to your ghost story. Are you thinking what I'm thinking about the deer in the mist that we saw last night?"

"I knew you'd be excited," said Max. "As soon as I read the story, I knew it had to be the same white deer we saw. I think Virginia Dare paid us a personal visit."

"It's got to be her," I said. "What do they want? What do the girl and the White Doe want me to do? I sure do wish they'd communicate better. And what do the girl and Virginia Dare and the ghost deer have to do with each other? You know, I think the little girl I saw hurrying in the woods with the woman might be Virginia Dare. It would make sense that little Virginia Dare is trying to get our attention anyway she can–whether as a child or as a white doe. What does she need from me?"

"Whoa, partner. You're firing questions left and right. I guess she'll let you know when she's good and ready. Seems like you can't hurry the mystery process."

Petey had listened attentively to the stories all night. He woofed his agreement with Max and then jumped out of my lap. Stretching, with his front down and his back end up in the air, he looked at the sky as the lightning flashed again.

"Storm's hitting, Jinx, Max. Time to go. Sleep now, and hunt tomorrow," Petey said.

We laughed in agreement and kicked sand into the fire pit just as the first fat drops of rain finished the job for us. The sky let loose, and we ran for our lives.

"Last one in has to carry the other two piggy back on the hike tomorrow," I shouted, as I exploded forward like a launching rocket.

"I just hope your back is strong enough. I weigh a couple hundred pounds in my hiking gear," panted Max, gaining on me.

Later that night, Petey told me that *some*thing made him stop running. He turned to look at the pile of boulders surrounded by mist in the warm rain. He wagged his tail, slowly at first, and then with all his might. The White Doe stepped out on the beach and bowed her regal head to Petey, before she disappeared once more in the mist.

Chapter Sixteen:

Petey Goes Missing

The morning dawned partly sunny. Stacks of black-laced nimbus clouds piled high in the distance, but the storms of the night had moved on.

Max and I finished our cereal and juice in his cottage kitchen and made our plans to search for the secret passageway. Both of us wore light jackets, jeans, thick socks, and our hiking-boots. We decided to start looking in the woods near the big pile of boulders close to our campfire.

"If the White Doe came to us there, she might be telling us it's a good place to start the search," Max said.

"Yes, there's something about that location that fits into the Big Mystery," I replied. "Remember how every evening Mom feels the strangeness there? I think it's so strong that even she knows something magical is going on."

Max's mother came into the kitchen and smiled at the two of us with our heads together. She looked pretty in a green tee shirt and pleated khaki shorts.

"You two look serious for a summer morning. Lighten up. Whatever you're trying to figure out will work out. Max has been telling me all about the Lost Colony."

"Yeah, Mom, we're going hiking today. We got a clue from some old legend that the colonists may have escaped an Indian attack through some underground tunnel. Wouldn't it be cool if we could find it?"

"Yes, it would be really cool Max, but don't go crawling underground. That wouldn't be cool. It would be very dangerous," said Mrs. Myers. "Besides, this is an island, no caves here.

She pulled the curtain aside and looked up at the clouds. "And be careful on your hike. They're still calling for more storms later today, so watch the sky and get home on the double if you see lightning. Your dad had to go back to the mainland to meet with some people from the office. I hope he doesn't get stuck there over night."

She looked a bit worried but smiled at us when she was left the kitchen. "Good luck clue hunting. Use your common sense."

Max shook his head and shrugged his shoulders. "My mom is the same as yours–no imagination," he said.

It was a good thing that we had on our jackets and jeans as we headed out. The air held a damp and cooler feel than it had in recent days. Petey ran ahead and we headed along the woods' edge toward the campfire pit.

"Let's run, let's run. You're too slow. Gotta look for that tunnel. Oh, the White Doe says start here," Petey said.

"Pete-o, have you been talking to ghosts again?" Max asked him.

But Petey had already dashed into the woods behind the boulders. We started off at a fast trot, trying to keep him in sight.

"Not so fast, Buddy. We only have two legs," I called after him.

We hiked further into the woods than we had before. A small, tangled path wove itself amongst the dense wooded area. Vines and prickly low brush scattered along the path grabbed at our ankles and threatened to trip us up as we followed the path.

Dark and cooler yet in the woods, we still worked up a good sweat in the humidity. We didn't remove our sweatshirts, though. We needed their protection. Gnats and pesky mosquitoes buzzed around our heads, and we had to keep swatting them away from our eyes.

Max reached into his backpack and handed me some bug spray. "Here," he said. "Use some of this, and spray your clothes, too. Those little buggers bite right through clothes." I thanked him, impressed again with his thoughtfulness in planning ahead.

After about half an hour I said, "Max, I don't think we should go in too much farther. We don't want to get lost."

"Don't worry, I've got my compass. We're heading southwest, so when we want to head back we follow the compass northeast. That will take us out of the woods to the beach area near our cottages."

Petey ran out of sight, but we could hear his excited little woofs up ahead. He seemed to be hot on the trail of something. I hoped it was some squirrels he chased after and not some big, fuzzy bear.

"Max, there aren't bears here on the island, are there?"

Max bared his teeth, his fingers hooked like bear claws, and he roared.

"All right, make fun of your detective partner. I hope the bear gets you first," I said. I made ferocious bear growls back at him.

We trotted on after Petey. That's when it happened. A hidden root tripped me. I went down with a crash, head first. My hands went out to break my fall, and I felt the painful jolt as I hit the ground.

"Oomph,! Ouch!" I yelled.

"Jinx, what happened? Are you all right?" Max called out, as he headed back down the small hill. Petey came running back and licked my face in concern.

I sat up in slow motion to check out the damage. "I don't think there's anything broken, just my injured pride. How could I be so stupid? I was looking so hard for an opening in the bank of the hill that I forgot to check my footing. Oh...ouch! That hurts."

My right ankle and both knees burned, but when I tried to move my left arm, some serious jolts of pain went through my wrist. Not a good sign.

"Let me see," Max said.

He stabilized my left arm and carefully felt it, starting at my shoulder. When he got to my wrist, the little squeeze he gave it caused another burst of pain.

"Owe!" I said through clenched teeth. "Doctor, I think you located the injured area. Don't touch it again."

"Now, now, don't get crabby," Max replied. "You patients always overreact in an emergency."

He flipped open his back pack and got out a semi-thawed juice box from our lunch bag.

"Hold this on your wrist to help lessen the swelling. I need to go look for a couple of thick sticks to use as splints to stabilize your wrist. Then I guess we better head back."

The wind began to pick up in strength. It rustled treetops and turned leaves silverside out. We looked skyward and saw dark clouds move in quickly. A loud rumble of thunder rolled over us, and the little hairs on the back of my neck stood up.

"Oh great, just what we needed, me injured in the woods like a dummy, during a raging thunderstorm threatening to drown us." I bit my lip–hard, and my shoulders slumped. "Sorry, Max."

"Jinx, it could just as easily have been me that tripped. Don't beat yourself up," Max said. He patted my shoulders awkwardly, then pointed to an outcropping. "Stay put, over there in that little overhang in the bank. It's safer than sitting under a large tree in a thunderstorm. Then you would be a dummy. I'll be right back."

He took off to search for the sticks to make the splint, and Petey and I wiggled back in under the bank. It had an overhang of dirt, moss, roots, and stone. It felt like I was in an earthen, protective hut.

Vivid lightning flashed closer. A giant clap of thunder followed. The last thing I remember thinking as my ears rang from the noise was, *"Hurry back here Max, this storm's going to be a whopper..."*

It was very, very dark. I still heard a faint ringing in my ears when I opened my eyes. I looked around for Orville, thinking he had something to show me, but he wasn't there.

Then, I realized I could see my colonial woman and her little girl in a cozy cabin room, sitting on a rough wooden bench by a crackling fire. Some lightning flashed outside their window, but they sat safe and warm by the fire. They laughed and sang, playing a game of Patty Cake. I felt their love for each other.

When the lightning flashed again, the mother said, "I wish Papa would return from hunting. The storm seems to be getting very close."

The lightning illuminated a dark form huddled outside their window, and I caught my breath. There crouched the tall, stern Indian I had seen in my previous vision in the woods. Again, it was obvious than unbeknownst to the mother and daughter, he watched the two with great interest, again.

To distract the child from the loud thunder, the woman got up and went to a wooden trunk bound in iron. She opened the latch and said, "Ginny, I want to give you something special. You are my big girl now, and I think the time is right to give you this present."

The little girl clapped her tiny hands together in happiness.

"Mama, a present!"

Lifting a wrapped parcel out of the trunk, the mother came back to the small child.

"Your Grand Papa John will be so proud to see how you have grown since his departure. He wanted to give this to you himself upon his return from England, but some matter seems to have delayed him." The mother had a sad look when she mentioned Grand Papa John, but she looked away so the little child couldn't see it.

Little Ginny took the package from her mother and tore off the paper. Her small hands shook, she was so excited. Inside was a beautiful wooden doll, dressed in a long skirt and apron. A tiny cap perched on the doll's head.

"Mama, the doll is from Grand Papa?" the girl asked.

"Yes, my precious daughter. It's from your Grand Papa. He ordered it from Germany, and he packed it to come to our new home here in America. He wanted to give it to you when you were old enough to take special care of it."

"I'm almost three, Mama. I'm a big girl now. I will love the doll from my Grand Papa. Her name will be Mary." The child gave it a kiss and rocked it in her arms.

Lightning flashed again outside their cabin door, and rain began to fall in torrents. The Indian turned away from the cabin and disappeared into the dark shadows.

Jinx, Jinx..." Max shook my shoulder. "Wake up now. I'm back. Are you ok?"

He was soaked, and his blond hair was plastered to his forehead. His blue eyes were troubled when I shook myself and tried to think straight.

The lightning flashed, and thunder roared overhead. The wind screamed and howled around our little shelter.

"This is a bad one Jinx. These winds have got to be gale force. We'd better ride this one out right here under cover."

Rain blew sideways past the front of our tiny shelter, and every once in a while it blew in on us with a gust. A giant tree toppled to our right, with a loud crash. Its leafy branches smashed into the ground in front of us.

"Petey, where's Petey?" I suddenly yelled to Max, against the roar of the wind and rain.

"Petey? I thought he was with you when I took off."

Our eyes desperately searched through the heavy rain and whipping, twisting low shrubbery.

"Petey...*Peee-teeey!*" I tried to get up to bolt into the woods in search of him, but Max grabbed my good arm.

"Wait until I splint your wrist, Jinx. When the storm lets up a bit, we'll both go get him. Petey's very smart. He's in under a safe rock like us, waiting out the worst of the storm."

Max was right, but I still worried myself sick. I don't know what I'd do if anything ever happened to Petey. *Jinx, get a grip,* I told myself. *Think...slow down... breathe slowly.*

Max tore a strip off the bottom of his T-shirt and tied the sticks to my arm for support. I pulled Orville's red silk bandanna out of my pocket and fingered it hopefully as a good luck charm. Then Max used it to make a sling for my arm.

I told him about the vision. "I wasn't asleep, Max. I was back in time again. I saw the cabin of the colonial lady and her little girl. I saw them plain as day and heard every word they said. She called the little girl Ginny. She gave her a doll, a present from her Grand Papa John. The same Indian I had seen in the woods watched them from outside their cabin. I'm afraid of him...I'm afraid he'll hurt them."

Max looked at me in amazement, his mouth wide open and his eyes startled and worried. "Jinx, I left you alone only a minute. You couldn't possibly have been anywhere but here. Now don't go weird on me."

Jinx described it all to Max, again. "I know what I saw. It's one of my time travel episodes. Like the ones you experienced. Everything is starting to come together. The colonial mother I keep seeing is Eleanor White Dare, with her little daughter, Virginia. Exactly like we thought. And the grandfather they talked about has to be Governor John White."

This time Max nodded slowly. "Yeah, okay. That makes sense, he replied. "You said the mother mentioned the grandfather not having returned from England. Holy mackeral! You've done it Jinx. You've figured out who they are."

"I think I know what happened when they hurried through the woods, too," I said thoughtfully. "They were in danger and ran away to hide. Maybe they got left behind when Manteo helped the colonists escape from the attack. Remember in that legend of the tunnel and cave, Ananias stayed behind to look for them."

I smacked my forehead with my good hand. "Good grief! It's taken me long enough to figure this out. All these clues practically put themselves together, and I still didn't get it, until now. Anyway, Virginia wanted to go back for some reason, but Eleanor told her they mustn't go back. Virginia had been very sad. I remember I had tears on my face for her."

Around us, the storm began to lessen. The sharp lightning and cracks of thunder were fewer, but the rain continued to pummel the trees and pound the ground in fury. I felt an overwhelming need to move on and search for Petey.

"Why does Virginia want your help, I wonder," said Max.

"Omigosh! I think we're about to find out," I whispered as I glanced out. "Look there beside the fallen tree. Do you see what I see?"

"Yes, I see it..." Max breathed it so silently, that I couldn't tell if he said it aloud or thought it to me.

A ground fog had sprung up when the cold air of the storm mixed with the warm, moist air of the forest. The rain lessened a bit more to a gentle pattering.

Out of the swirling mist, from behind the tower of fallen limbs and green leaves, stepped the White Doe.

Chapter Seventeen:

Help At Last

The White Doe stood in the swirling mist, more beautiful and delicate than anything I've ever seen. Max and I slowly, and quietly, crawled out of our shelter and stood almost spellbound under the gaze of her gentle eyes.

The sun broke out of the clouds and shone down through the leaves, highlighting the spot where she stood. She absolutely dazzled in the sunlight as she took a few steps toward us. As quick as the blink of an eye, she transformed into a young girl about my age, dressed in a long, white gown. I knew exactly who she was–she looked like an older version of little Virginia Dare. I thought I caught the glimpse of wings. She smiled sadly at us.

"I lost my doll long ago. She was a gift from my Grand Papa. Please, help me find it...her name is Mary," she said, and a tear rolled down her beautiful face. "I want to take Mary home with me."

The fog swirled and dissipated in the warmth of the sun, and the young maiden was gone like a wish on the wind. Max and I stood transfixed in silence. Then I turned to him.

"We know what she wants now, but I still don't know how to help her," I said quietly. "Where on earth would we find her doll? If it even still exists after all this time."

Max shrugged his shoulders and shook his head. "I don't know either, but we'll think of something," said Max.

He took my right hand and started walking away from our shelter. "It's time to find Petey. Maybe he'll know what to do," Max said.

We walked through the woods, still following the faint trail. After fifteen or twenty minutes of softly calling for Petey, we stopped for a drink of juice and a sandwich out of the backpack.

My wrist throbbed, but the fear of losing Petey hurt more. In the strange silence of the woodland afternoon, with everything soaked from the storm, we suddenly heard gentle woofing. I finally knew Petey was ok.

"This way, Max. He sounds fine, but that's his 'guarding something' bark," I called back over my shoulder. I took off at a run, up the rising terrain.

"Hey partner, not too fast. Next you'll fall and break a leg, and I'll have to drag you out of here by the armpits. That won't be a pretty picture." Max said.

We crested the hill and found Petey. He lay by some rocks near a few trees. At first my heart thundered in my chest, because I thought he was injured. Then I could see he was protecting a small, washed out area. The rain must have carried away some of the earth around the rocks, and Petey lay beside the rocks with a paw protectively over the hole.

Petey was dirty, bedraggled, and soaking wet, but we were so glad to see him that we both scooped him up in our arms. He licked our faces and wiggled to get down.

"Petey, you had us so worried," I scolded. "Why did you go off like that, without telling anyone?"

"You were safe. The girl called for help."

"What on earth are you talking about? What girl? Virginia dare?"

Petey led us back to the washed out area beside the rocks. *"Ginny was afraid. I watched over her."*

Petey looked from us back to the hole, wagged his stubby tail, and lay down again.

"Ginny is safe now. It's time for you to help her find her doll," Petey said.

I stared at Petey, amazed again by how much he knew but never told me.

Max and I peered cautiously into the hole that had been exposed by the heavy rainstorm. When I saw what was in there, I couldn't hold back a loud yelp. There, partially exposed in the dirt, rested some human bones and a skull. They were about the size of a teen, like Max and me. It seems like the Lost Colony wasn't lost any more. They had become the found colony. Something happened to young Virginia Dare long ago, and we, apparently, stumbled upon her final resting place.

"Oh no, no, no," I said. "This is too much–even for the *JMP History Mystery Detective Agency*. A skeleton? No! Max, let's get out of here. I've had enough."

I held my throbbing arm against my chest and scrambled frantically backwards, away from the collection of bones.

Petey barked in alarm, and Max yelled, "Jinx, stop. You'll fall down the bank..."

Just before I took that last step backwards, I felt the firm pressure of two sturdy hands on my back. Someone gently prodded me forward, back toward safe ground. Startled, I looked wild-eyed at Max and Petey. Petey wagged his whole body in excitement, but Max stood in shocked silence.

I looked behind me. There he stood, tall and silent. My Indian Brave that had been in my visions towered over us. He had his arms crossed in front of his chest, his head tilted, and he watched me curiously with his coal black eyes.

I turned back to see if Max was really seeing what I was and caught a glimmer of Orville, standing beside Max. Orville was finally dressed in his old-fashioned suit, holding his hat in his hand. He nodded and smiled at Max and me, and then with a two-finger salute, he disappeared. I think he felt his duty to help me was finished.

I gulped and looked back at the Indian. I remembered the first time that I had seen him hiding behind the tree, secretly watching Eleanor and little Virginia, when I felt cold fear. Now, I knew that I had nothing to fear from this Indian. He hadn't meant them any harm, and this time he saved me from another bad fall.

The Indian had bright paint smeared on his bronzed cheeks and arms. He slowly placed one open hand on his chest and said, "I am Wanchese. I am the weroance of my tribe of Roanoacs. I will not harm you. You must help the young white girl. Now come quickly with me."

Max and I closed our mouths and nodded our heads silently. Wanchese! Max had to have known right away who the Indian was–he had been Wanchese in his journey to the past.

I had actually met Manteo's former blood brother. We had no choice but to follow this Indian Brave. We quickly covered the gravesite with some branches for protection, then started off behind him.

Wanchese led us on, away from the path and deeper into the wooded area. Max and I glanced at each other in nervous silence as we followed him, but Petey trotted by the Indian's side looking very perky and excited.

"Petey sure has the strangest friends," Max mumbled, grimly. I nodded in agreement.

The air shimmered, and that persistent strange mist floated around Wanchese and Petey, Max, and me.

The world looked out of focus. I had a hard time determining whether we were in our present or had shifted to Wanchese's past.

We soon came to another rocky, hilly area surrounded by loblolly pine and oak trees. The Brave squatted down, and with all his might, he shoved and pushed a medium sized rock away from an opening in a dirt bank. An earthy smelling air filtered out of the opening. I could see it led back further underground.

"Max," I breathed, "it's a tunnel. We've found the underground passage. Maybe it's the Lost Colony's escape route."

We didn't even think about our promise of not going into any cave when we scrambled through the opening on our stomachs. We *had* to go into the cave.

It was a tight squeeze for the large Indian, but Max and I had no trouble at all. The tunnel went on about thirty feet, then opened up into a small, rocky room. Faint light filtered from somewhere above.

We struggled to our feet, and Max pulled a flashlight out of his beloved backpack. I marveled again at how prepared my buddy was for every kind of emergency.

Wanchese watched with curious interest as Max flicked on the flashlight. The room shone in brightness.

The Brave cocked his head and said, "Hmmm...*good* fire stick."

He almost grinned before his face returned to its stern expression. But I could see the twinkle of amusement and wonderment in his eyes.

I stared around in amazement. I had never been in a cave before and thought they were always dank and dripping wet. This cave had a dry dirt floor, and its rocky walls and ceiling must have been carved by a water source that long ago evaporated.

Max shined his flashlight slowly over the walls. The Indian went over to a notch that had been chiseled into one side. He removed a small, metal box about the size of a shoebox and handed it to us.

"The white child is so sad. She dropped her precious gift long ago as she ran through the forest. I saved it for her. Now you must return it to her so her spirit can fly away home," Wanchese said.

When I lifted the lid I saw a wooden doll dressed in an old-fashioned gown and apron. Her tiny cap came down over her ears, tied in a bow. Even though a bit dusty, with the painted features on her face faded, I still knew it was Virginia's doll from her Grand Papa.

"Oh, Max! This is the doll I saw in the vision. This is what she wanted to go back for." I found myself blinking back tears. "Her mother must have told her it was too dangerous to turn back."

"Poor kid," said Max. "The only thing she had to help her remember her grandfather, and she lost it. Can you imagine how frightened and sad she must have been?"

"You go now," said the Indian. "Follow your little dog. He knows the way."

We turned to say good-bye, but the kind-hearted Wanchese was gone.

Petey led us directly back to the place where we had left Virginia's skeleton. Along the way, Max kept looking at me.

"Are you ok? Do you need to stop for a rest? How's the wrist doing?" he said.

"I appreciate the concern Max, but you are starting to sound like a little old nurse maid. Let's just keep going. We need to get this doll back to Virginia. She's waited four hundred years for it."

Max grinned at me. "Now I know you're ok," he said, "because you're grumpy again.

I stopped, grabbed his arm, and looked him in the eyes.

"I really do thank you for helping me. I don't think Petey and I could have handled all of this strange adventure without you. You always know just what to do."

"Oh gosh," Max replied. "I'll bet you tell that to all of your detective assistants."

But I could tell he appreciated the compliment.

We soon reached the gravesite and approached the branches that covered it, all undisturbed, as we had left it. I carefully uncovered the bones. This time they didn't frighten me. They just made me feel sad.

I took a deep breath and said, "Max, I want you to help me place this doll beside the bones. Somehow, that feels like the right thing to do."

We held the doll between us, and together, we placed it by the small pile of bones. Suddenly, it was as if we couldn't let go of the doll.

Our arms began shaking, and I felt a cool tingling from the tips of my fingers all the way up my arm. Then the doll simply disappeared.

"Ohmigosh!" I whispered.

"Uh, yeah. Me, too," Max hissed.

We looked up in surprise and saw Virginia standing near by, again. She held her precious doll in her arms.

Virginia smiled widely and said, "Thank you, friends. Thank you." Then she tilted her head and looked off in the distance. "Yes, Mama, I'm coming."

The cool tingling sensation faded, and our young friend from the past disappeared into the misty afternoon. This time I knew she was gone for good. We had freed Virginia to fly away home.

Chapter Eighteen:

Summer Flies By

"Jinx! Max! Can you hear us?" We heard our mothers' voices calling out to us. They were on the search and rescue trail, and they meant business.

"Up here, Mom. At the top of the hill, by the rocks," I shouted. I had never heard anything as sweet as my mom's voice.

They charged up the hill through the thick underbrush and stopped short when they spotted us. We looked like a dirty, tattered mess.

Max's mom looked about ready to cry. She heaved a big sigh of relief. "Oh, kids," she said. "I'm so glad we finally found you. When the storm came up so suddenly and you didn't return home, we were terrified that something bad had happened to you." Her attention shifted to me. "Jinx, your arm–you've hurt yourself."

My mother came over to me and checked out my wrist with gentle fingers.

"I tripped myself up, Mom. My arm really throbbed with pain, at first. But Max iced it with a frozen juice box and splinted it for me. It really doesn't feel too bad, now. Didn't he do a great job?" I smiled at my partner.

"Max, you *are* a good friend," Mom said. She gave him a hug. "Thanks so much for the excellent first-aid help." Max's ears got beet red, but he grinned from ear to ear.

I worried about how much of this adventure we should tell our mothers. They both warned us not to go into any caves, and I wasn't up for a lecture right now.

"Max, trust me to handle this. You can tell your mom as much as you need to later," I silently communicated to him.

"Good idea, partner. Take it away," he returned.

"Mom, we managed to get in under shelter during the worst of the storm, but Petey went off exploring on his own. He found something that I need to show you."

We walked over to Virginia's resting place. As both moms knelt to peer into the hole, I could see they were shocked into silence. The doll was gone. I glanced at Max. He winked at me and touched his finger to his lips.

Mom, being an archeologist, immediately began to closely inspect the bones.

"These are a human child's bones," she said in surprise. " It's an older child, maybe a teen. I can tell from their appearance that they are very old. You did well not to touch them. I'll report them to the leaders at the archeological dig site. They'll be excited to examine them."

"Then what will happen to them, Mrs. MacKenzie?" asked Max.

We both worried about that. After all, they belonged to a real girl that we knew. It wasn't like they were some ancient rock specimens.

"They'll be studied very carefully and handled with great respect," said Mom. "We'll be able to learn many things about them, like how old they are, whether it's a boy or a girl, and even whether they are the bones of a Native American or English child. Then they will be laid in a final resting place–maybe in that little church graveyard further inland."

"That would be nice, if it's a pretty, grassy place with lots of trees," I murmured.

Mrs. Myers clapped her hands and took charge. "Let's get these storm refugees cleaned up and into warmer clothes," she said. "Then we can hike back home and get Jinx's wrist checked at the clinic. You two detectives are keeping the emergency room busy this summer, aren't you? Let's hope this is the last time we have to visit there, eh?"

She reached into a backpack, very much like the one Max dragged around, and pulled out dry sweatshirts and big, fluffy beach towels. "I even packed hot chocolate and homemade oatmeal cookies. We all need some energy right now."

Then Mrs. Myers really got things going. She grabbed Petey in a towel, rubbed and fluffed his fur, and dried him off. Petey closed his eyes and raised his head so she could reach his neck and chest. He looked like he was in pure bliss. Next, she rubbed us dry, fluffed our hair like she did with Petey's, handed us warm sweatshirts, and poured us sweet, hot chocolate, all at one time, it seemed.

I burst out laughing.

"What?" inquired Max and his mom, both at the same time.

"Now I know where Max gets his "Be Prepared" training," I said. "We scatterbrained, disorganized people really appreciate people like you."

"That's right, kiddo. Our motto is 'think ahead,' isn't it Max?"

"Right, Mom," laughed Max, and he gave his mother a huge hug. "You always say 'the Lord helps those that help themselves.'"

We drank the hot chocolate and thanked Max's mom with hugs, while Mom marked off the area to secure it. Finally, we hiked back down the path, careful not to slip in the mud. Petey led the pack with his head lifted high in the air and a spring in his trot. He had done his job very well.

The rest of the summer went faster than even seemed possible. My broken wrist felt much better in a few weeks. Max and I talked often about all of the strange happenings, reliving the events and trying to make sense of it all. Our brains still couldn't quite process what happened, and how our lives have changed. I knew the Big Mystery had all been put to rest, because no more midnight visitors or visions of long ago made their way into our dreams.

Most of the time we were just two happy kids and a furry dog, playing and swimming at the beach. We finally got to go surfing again by August–head healed, arm healed. I really started to get the hang of it! Who would have thought–Jinx MacKenzie, Surfer Dude-ette!

We each talked to our mothers alone. They accepted our stories pretty well. Max talked with his Mom and Dad more about his family's special gifts. I told Mom everything, even about crawling in the tunnel and cave. Instead of lecturing me, she hugged me when I spilled out the whole story. She told me she knew that I was special the day I was born.

Mom explained how the gifts I had were inherited from our ancestors. My great grandmother, my grandmother, and Mom all had psychic gifts to a certain extent. Mom said her power was seeing into the future, and it had weakened, as she got older.

She also told me my Aunt Merry had powers very much like mine. I couldn't wait for my next visit with her. She'd been holding out important information on me!

It helped to know I wasn't alone with all of this. I had Max for a friend, now, too. He told me he found out that his family's gifts were the same as mine, only it was the men in his family who passed on the gift.

Wow! Happy teenage-birthday to me! We all celebrated it with birthday cake on the beach. The biggest gift of all was my own gift to me–the ability to time travel and help others back in time.

In July, I typed up my paper about the Lost Colony. My theory supported the idea of Manteo helping the colonists escape to his inland village during a hostile Indian attack. I didn't mention meeting my kind Indian Brave, Wanchese, or helping Virginia recover her doll.

However, I did include the *Legend of the White Doe* in my paper. I couldn't resist mentioning that we spotted what appeared to be a pure white deer on Roanoke Island. I had to put some of our mysterious adventure into my report. Let the readers decide what was real and what were misty stories told long ago around the campfire. I did my best to keep the legend alive.

Max walked along with Petey and me one day in August when I got my grade on the research paper at the Post Office. I was so nervous about the grade that I gave the letter to Max to open. He tried to look shocked and mad, like it was bad news, but I could see right through that act. We did the happy dance with Petey and gave each other "high fives" all the way back home.

Mom and Dad were so proud of me when they read the teacher's comments. She wrote, *"This is the best student research paper I have ever read. Jinx made this historical event and the first English colonists come alive with her carefully planned out paper and commentary. It sounded like she was right there with them! A+."* *If she only knew,* I thought. I was proud, too.

The archeologists' preliminary report pretty much confirmed that the bones were the remains of a white young female, dated at around four hundred years old. They would never know that the bones belonged to Virginia Dare. That secret would remain with Max, Petey, and me.

Epilogue:

Saying Good-bye

And so ended the best summer of my life. I had learned a valuable lesson about dry, boring old history. My new motto is *"Real People-Real History!"* I gained a great respect for those folks of long ago. I hoped that I could live my life with half of the same hopes, dreams, and ambitions that they had for making this world a better place. I learned that I owe them *that* much.

Max and I met for hotdogs and S'mores on our last evening together. Tomorrow Max and his family would return to their home in New York. Mom, Petey and I would soon head home to Pennsylvania to be with Dad. School was right around the corner. I found myself hoping that I had a double period of seventh grade history. I'm ready to find some other history mysteries to solve.

We decided to build a last campfire at our favorite location. The sunset glowed in a burst of purples and scarlet reds all around us. Soon the fire crackled and spit embers into the air, and a million stars twinkled like fireflies and lit the night sky.

We sat for quite a while in silence, comfortable in each other's company. Petey snuggled in Max's lap, forlornly gazing into Max's blue eyes like he was losing his last friend.

"Pete-o," Max said, "I think I'll have to steal you from Jinx and smuggle you home in my suitcase."

"I love you Max. I'm sad. I'll miss you," Petey sighed.

"I love you too, buddy. What am I going to do without my two sidekicks? I feel like I've known you forever. We've been through a lot together this summer."

"Max, do you know the first time I saw you on the ferry I thought you were really cute?" I confessed.

"Yeah?" Max laughed. "Well guess what? I thought you were really cute, too. I still do. I'll miss you the most."

He stretched over, accidentally dumping Petey onto the sand, and gave me a kiss on the cheek.

"Sorry, buddy," he said to Petey as he scooped him back into his lap. "I...um...got carried away."

I could tell that he was *sooo* embarrassed.

"Now don't be getting all mushy on me, Maxwell M. Myers." I said.

A kiss, I thought. *Omigosh! I just got my first boy kiss, and I really liked it.* Now *my* ears were red.

"We joke about our meeting each other being fate," I said. "But I really believe we were meant to use our special gifts of time travel and communicating with people from the past together. We're a pretty powerful force as a team. It's only just begun, too."

Max scratched a mosquito bite on his ankle and turned to me again. "I know you're right, Jinx. We'll be called upon soon to help with another situation in the past. I feel it in here." He tapped his chest with his fist.

"This one taught us so much about the Native American's and their point-of- view. It was a hard time for them and the English colonists. Like Orville said, 'And so it begins...' He meant the Spanish and English explorers and colonists were the first to treat the Native Americans so horribly. No wonder the Indians fought back. And it continues even today. Life on the Indian reservations is really poor." I gave a giant sigh.

We stared into the glowing embers without talking for a few minutes.

"We solved lots of mysteries together, didn't we?" Max said. "We figured out the colonial woman and the girl were Eleanor Dare and Virginia, the very first English baby born in America. Oh, yeah, I read that soon after Virginia's birth, another baby was born."

"Really? Oh, no! So many missing men and women, and now another child...I hope they lived happily and had a good life in Manteo's village." It really bothered me that children were dragged along into this hard new life their parents had decided to try, without having any voice in the decision.

"Max, we also connected the beautiful white doe in the mist to the *Legend of the White Doe.* Young Virginia Dare, who was turned into a white doe, to be forever banned to Roanoke Island by the evil medicine man, Chico," I added. "That is so sad, and sooo romantic,"

I added. I placed my hands over my heart and watched the fire spit little sparks into the air like miniature fireworks.

Max couldn't help it–he snorted and grinned at me. "Okay–definitely a girl moment. Moving on... We solved the two biggest mysteries of all, what did Virginia Dare want, and what happened to the Lost Colony. Not bad for a couple of kids new to this time-traveling stuff, huh?" he said.

Then, I got very serious and looked down into the embers of the fire. "I think the biggest lesson I learned was not to judge someone by their looks. I really was scared of Wanchese when I saw how stealthy he was, watching Eleanor and Virginia, covered in war paint. But, it turned out that he not only saved me, but he had a big heart for helping a little girl find her Grand Papa's missing present."

Petey snored on, and his paws twitched, like he chased sea gulls in his dreams. Max finally placed Petey in my lap and stood up, brushing the sand from his jeans.

Petey shook his head and opened his button eyes. *"What did I miss, what did I miss? Are we going home yet?"* he said, still a bit confused and sleepy.

"Almost bedtime, Petey," I said. I stroked his face, so precious to me.

"Well, I guess I'll head back to the cottage," Max said. "Are you ready to put out the fire?"

I shook my head no. I wasn't ready for this campfire to be over quite yet. I wanted to stay, alone with Petey, and just *feel* the mist and smoke, and hear the lapping water of the sound, and totally inhale the pine scent in the beach air.

"I think Petey and I will stay here a bit longer. We'll run over to your cottage tomorrow morning to say a final good bye." I smiled up at Max, my newest, best friend, after all we had experienced together. A tight bond was forged this summer, and we both felt it.

Max snapped his fingers. "Oh, yeah, I almost forgot." He flipped open his back pack and reached inside. "I found this at a gift shop in Manteo the other day, when Mom and I shopped for souvenirs. As soon as I saw it I saw it, I knew right away I had to get it for you."

He handed me a rumpled package wrapped in bright blue tissue paper and covered with scotch tape.

"Sorry," he mumbled, "I'm not much of a gift wrapper."

I eagerly tore into the tissue paper. A small, old-fashioned looking colonial doll, identical to Virginia's doll, lay in my hands.

I jumped up and gave him a big hug. "It's perfect! It's the best present I ever got. I'll name her Mary."

Max broke away first and tugged at that curl behind his ear. "Ok then. Um...I'll say good night, Jinx. See you tomorrow morning, Petey."

Max gave a brisk wave and trotted off over the sand toward his cottage. At the top of the last dune, he turned around and cupped his hands around his mouth.

"Jinx," he called, "you'll text me, won't you?"

"You bet, partner." I said. "Maybe we can even telecommunicate through the air. We've got to practice that, because I have a gut feeling that the *JMP History Mystery Detective Agency* is going to be needed again in the near future."

Max gave me a thumbs-up and disappeared over the crest of the dune.

"Nooooo, no more mysteries. I need to sleep," Petey said, grumpily.

I hugged my hairy little guy. "No more mysteries to solve right now, Petey. You deserve a good rest. Job well done."

All was secure in my world.

"Just let me tell you a nice story," I comforted him. I gazed dreamily into the glowing coals.

"Walk this way, History Fans. It was a dark and stormy night...."

THE END

Appendix I

A Letter to My Readers

Dear Readers,

I hope you enjoyed ***White Doe in the Mist.*** You are the reason I write–to share Real People and Real History with you, along with the terrific adventures of the ***JMP*** Gang!

The main characters in the story, Jinx, Max, Petey, and their parents are wonderful people who are the product of my imagination. However, the story of ***The Lost Colony*** that Jinx's mom told the teens is true.

Many scholars have researched it over the past four hundred years, and to this day there is no definitive answer to the mystery. What really happened to those brave colonists? How could ninety-one men, seventeen women, and nine children disappear without a trace into the misty air of Roanoke Island in the Outer Banks of North Carolina?

Sir Richard Grenville's attack on the village of Aquascococke over the matter of a missing silver cup is true, recorded in history. The Indians' whole village, along with their cornfields, was burned to the ground. The mystery of the missing silver cup was not solved. It was also recorded that Ralph Lane led the attack that killed Wingina and his family, over a supposed plot by the Indians to attack his fort.

These attacks on the Native Americans badly affected the relationships between the two different groups.

The stories of the White Doe, and the escape from hostile Indians through tunnels and caves, were handed down through the years as ***legends*** told around the campfire. Many ***legends*** began as accounts of true stories, and as the years pass and oral histories are passed down, facts are forgotten or changed to make the story more exciting, until often the real truth is lost in time.

I encourage you to visit my favorite place in the whole world: Roanoke Island and the Outer Banks of North Carolina. Find Wilbur and Orville's monument on the sand dune. Climb Jockey's Ridge and hang-glide from the top (Petey will want to go with you!) Visit the wonderful museum at

Festival Park on Roanoke Island that tells the story of the Lost Colony, and scramble on board the replica flagship, ***Elizabeth II*** to explore life aboard a sailing ship. Best of all, visit the actual earthwork remains of the original Fort Raleigh uncovered by archeologists.

Warning! There is a very strange feeling in the air on Roanoke Island. If you watch very carefully, you may spot the ***White Doe*** back in the forest, or little Virginia Dare may want to show you her doll.

Oh, yes, ***Blackbeard the Pirate*** may want to speak with you, so watch your golden coins and jewels... but that's another story.

Happy reading,

Faith Reese Martin

PS: Please come visit me on my website at: **www.faithreesemartin.com**, or write to me at: **ghostwriterfm@verizon.net**

Appendix II

Glossary:

Appendix III

Real Characters to Research

Appendix IV

Places to Visit:

Appendix V

Queen Elizabeth and the Tudors of England